Holding C... **n**
was the mo... **e**
ordering o... **d**
ver experie...

Already he was hurtling close to the edge of that self-imposed control. He knew he shouldn't want her so much. This had disaster written all over it.

With a supreme test of will Jake slid his hands up to Caitlin's shoulders, where he briefly let them linger. Then he gently but firmly moved er away. Her eyes instantly registered surprise and confusion, and Jake cursed himself for orturing them both.

'I don't want to hurt you,' he murmured.

Caitlin bit her lip and inclined her head in a brief nod. Then she turned back, crossing her arms over her chest as if to protect herself. Her beautiful hair cascaded down her back like the most luxurious black silk and Jake ached with every fibre of his being to reach out and touch it. He had been captivated by women before, but not like this—*never* like this.

The day **Maggie Cox** saw the film version of *Wuthering Heights*, with a beautiful Merle Oberon and a very handsome Laurence Olivier, was the day she became hooked on romance. From that day onwards she spent a lot of time dreaming up her own romances, secretly hoping that one day she might become published and get paid for doing what she loved most!

Now that her dream is being realised she wakes up every morning and counts her blessings. She is married to a gorgeous man and is the mother of two wonderful sons. Her two other great passions in life—besides her family and reading/writing—are music and films.

Recent titles by the same author:

THE MAN SHE CAN'T FORGET
THE TYCOON'S DELICIOUS DISTRACTION
WHAT HIS MONEY CAN'T HIDE
DISTRACTED BY HER VIRTUE

Did you know these are also available as eBooks?
Visit www.millsandboon.co.uk

A RULE
WORTH BREAKING

BY
MAGGIE COX

Published in Great Britain 2014
by Mills & Boon, an imprint of Harlequin (UK) Limited,
Eton House, 18-24 Paradise Road, Richmond, Surrey, TW9 1SR

© 2014 Maggie Cox

ISBN: 978-0-263-90924-1

Harlequin (UK) Limited's policy is to use papers that are natural,
renewable and recyclable products and made from wood grown in
sustainable forests. The logging and manufacturing processes conform
to the legal environmental regulations of the country of origin.

Printed and bound in Spain
by Blackprint CPI, Barcelona

A RULE
WORTH BREAKING

To Joy
You were and always will be one of the true lights of my life.
With love and affection,
Maggie x

CHAPTER ONE

'WHAT DO YOU think?' Unable to suppress the disagreeable sense of disappointment that was churning in his gut, Jake Sorenson glanced up at the stage at Rick—his 'partner in crime'—who was all but wearing out the floor, pacing back and forth in his worn Cuban-heeled boots. *The auditions weren't exactly going well.*

Rick abruptly stopped pacing to spear an exasperated hand through his dull gold hair. Studying Jake, he snapped, 'What do I think? I think that Rosie Rhys-Jones, or whatever her name is, just isn't good enough. God knows Marcie is a hard act to follow, but *Rosie...*'

'Josie.'

'Josie. Whatever...' Scowling, Rick folded his muscular arms across his leather waistcoat and continued. 'The woman would be fine on a cruise ship, entertaining folk with more money than taste, but she's not lead vocalist material and that's a fact. Bottom line is, Jake, I can't see any of the singers we've heard so far fronting a potentially great band like Blue Sky—can you?'

In answer, Jake stared off into the distance. Mentally reviewing the past few auditions, he couldn't help but agree. He returned his arresting blue gaze to his friend and the characteristic dimple that highlighted a rare smile appeared at the side of his mouth.

'You're right, of course. We'll just have to keep on looking.'

Jake rarely elaborated. Not unless he absolutely had to.

But he knew that when it came to making a decision ultimately the final say would be his. Although Rick had been in the music business even longer than he had—at the height of his career Jake had been one of the most successful record producers in the business—he knew that the other man valued his expertise and judgement.

'Is there anyone left outside to see?' Yawning as he rose to his feet, Jake stretched his arms high above his head. The movement made his shirt ride up several inches to reveal a taut flat stomach tapering into lean hips and long-boned thighs, currently encased in faded dark blue denim.

At the same time Rick expertly jumped off the stage and ambled across the dusty wooden floor to join him. 'Not unless they're lurking in the graveyard out there' he joked.

He feigned an exaggerated shiver, his bemused expression conveying exactly what he thought about conducting auditions in an obscure village hall deep in the heart of rural England. But Jake knew that doing things this way at least afforded them a certain amount of privacy that wasn't always possible in London.

The music press and tabloids were always keen to know what he was up to. He was the man who had famously brought several acts from the UK to prominence. But at the height of his career he'd been caught up in a destructive scandal that had cut short his seemingly unstoppable rise to the top when it hit the headlines. After that Jake had dropped out of producing and promoting bands to lick his wounds, reassess his life and reflect on what he might do instead.

For a few years following his very public fall from grace he'd become a perpetual nomad, travelling the world. And while he'd thought he would never entertain the idea of working in the music industry again, when he'd been travelling he'd begun to listen to and study the ethnic music of other cultures and realised that he couldn't leave music alone. It had always been and still was his abiding interest—the thing that made life worth living. And when he'd finally brought his explorative sojourn to an end he'd returned to the UK and made the decision to go back to his roots.

He'd started out managing a band long before he'd become a producer and now, after fifteen years in the business, had come full circle to manage Blue Sky.

Glancing down at his watch, he grimaced. 'Anyway, I think I've heard enough to know that we haven't found our singer yet. Want to call it a day?'

Dropping his hands to his hips, Jake glanced across at the three band members who were waiting expectantly for him to make a decision about what they were going to do next.

'No doubt these guys have had enough, too. So let's go get a hot pie and a beer. We can make an early start in the morning. There's a girl from Birmingham that might be a possibility. She's lead vocalist in a band that have attracted quite a following in her home town'

Despite trying to sound hopeful, Jake knew his downbeat tone conveyed that the girl from Birmingham was more than likely another no. What he was looking for—what they were *all* looking for—was someone extraordinary, a girl who stood out from the crowd, who could hold her own fronting a band that had been on the brink of major success before Marcie's sudden and abrupt departure.

It was a crying shame that the woman should have decided at the eleventh hour that she'd rather marry her childhood sweetheart and go and cultivate grapes in the Dordogne than front a rock band. But that, as they said, was showbiz. Still, if anyone could work a miracle Jake knew that *he* could. All he needed to prove it was to find an amazing singer.

A door slammed loud and hard and the shock in the room was tangible. The sound reverberated round the vaulted high-ceilinged hall like a cannon exploding. *What the hell...?*

Jake was taken aback when he saw the perpetrator. Tall, slim and dark-haired, she was struggling with the belt of her raincoat, which he could see had become trapped be-

tween the hall's back doors when they'd slammed shut. His
transfixed gaze worked its way up from long black suede
boots to slim toned legs clad in sheer black hosiery. For a
long moment he was fixated by a shapely knee, where its
smooth flesh peeped intriguingly through a frayed tear the
size of a small coin. As she struggled to free her belt the girl
emitted a breathy little sound that might have been a curse.

Briefly turning his head, Jake found Rick grinning. *He
knew it wasn't just because the girl had got herself in a fix.*
When she finally extricated the belt and lifted her head to
murmur a blushing apology he felt as though all the air had
just been punched out of his lungs. *She was absolutely stunning.* Even at a distance he could see that her eyes were the
most dazzling emerald-green he'd ever seen in his life. Add
to that apple cheeks, and full, luscious lips stained the colour
of ripe cherries, and Jake sensed all the testosterone in the
room heave a collective sigh—his own included.

Rick was the first to recover. 'Hi. Can I help you?' he
called out cheerfully.

'This is where the auditions are being held, isn't it?'

Glancing nervously round her, the girl took in the five
men standing there, as well as the stacked plastic chairs lin-
ing the walls, the dusty floor and the lofty ceiling with its
yellowing cracked plasterwork. Her expression was definitely bemused, as if she couldn't quite believe where she'd
landed. She still hadn't moved any further away from the
door.

'Am I too late? I'm sorry I couldn't get here a bit earlier
but I've been stocktaking' Swiping a hand down her short
black skirt, she tugged the edges of her raincoat together in
front of it, as if she might have inadvertently displayed more
than she wanted to.

'Stocktaking, you say?' Rick's wolfish grin grew even
wider. 'You can check *my* stock any time you want to, honey.'

Time to take charge, Jake thought with a flash of irritation. The girl might be easy on the eye, but she was more

than likely another time-waster or wannabe—and God knew he'd auditioned enough of them in the past four days to be honestly weary of hearing any more.

To make matters worse, he'd *lived* with a girl just like that and she'd all but broken him with her relentless desire for fame and fortune. Not to mention what she'd been prepared to do to get it. *In any case, the girl in front of him probably couldn't sing for toffee.*

But even as his cynical gaze surveyed her he felt a hot flash of desire throb through him. He was almost dizzy with the power of it, and in that moment he saw it as a warning to steer well clear—because something told him that, given the chance, the allure of this incredible beauty would be too hard to resist.

The realisation that he might be tempted honestly scared him. Temptation was never a simple option. In Jake's book it equalled weakness, and he was a man who liked to be in control. From a young age he'd quickly intuited that if he didn't take care of himself and instigate boundaries then he was damn sure no one else would.

'Actually, you're too late.'

But even as the words left his lips he immediately belied them. Helplessly drawn, he found himself moving towards the bewitching woman, and somehow the necessity to get her to leave…and *quick*…melted clean away. All his instincts told him to take the chance to admire her beauty while he could. After all, it wasn't every day that a veritable *angel* presented herself in front of him…

'What I mean to say is' he went on 'is that you're too late for the auditions today but you can come back tomorrow if you're serious. If not, then all I can do is thank you for your interest and wish you well.'

'You're questioning if I'm serious or not? If I'm not serious about auditioning then why do you think I'm here?'

Surprised that she would come back at him like that, Jake sighed. His innate instinct was for self-preservation, and his mind scrambled to give her a legitimate reason why he couldn't let her audition today.

'Well, if that's the case, then you won't mind coming back tomorrow, will you? We've been auditioning since early this morning and we could all use a break,'

Watching her wrestle with the emotion his words must have wrought, he saw her hand tuck her hair behind her ear, then free it again as if she wasn't quite sure what to do next.

'I was really hoping you could hear me tonight. The thing is, I won't be able to make it tomorrow'

'Then you can't be that serious about auditioning, can you?'

Hot colour suffused her apple cheeks—but not because of embarrassment, Jake guessed. His cutting rejoinder had infuriated her.

Not wanting to be swayed by her angelic face and big green eyes, he told himself to stand firm. Nonetheless, he heard himself ask, 'What's your name?'

'It's Caitlin. Caitlin Ryan.'

'Well, Caitlin…' Folding his arms across his chest, he let his light-coloured gaze flick an interested glance up and down her figure, simply because it was too irresistible to ignore. 'Like I said, if you're serious about auditioning then you'll come back tomorrow, when it's more convenient for us to hear you. Shall we say around eleven-thirty?'

'I'm sorry…' The woman's incandescent emerald gaze was immediately perturbed. 'I don't want to be a nuisance, but I honestly can't make it tomorrow. A close friend—the manager of the shop where I work—is having her wisdom teeth removed, and I'm the only one who can stand in for her while she's away'

Jake fought down a compelling urge to laugh out loud. Of all the answers he might have expected her to furnish him with, the imminent removal of a friend's wisdom teeth hadn't been one of them!

He could almost sense Rick's laughter bubbling up behind him. *Damn*. It was going to be pretty hard to refuse this beauty anything when she was staring back at him like some little girl lost, those big green eyes of hers reflecting equal measures of hope and disappointment.

'Give the girl a break, man.' As he planted himself beside Jake Rick's amiable features creased into a persuasive smile. 'The band is still set up, so what have we got to lose?'

My sanity, for one thing, thought Jake, with grave misgiving. If Caitlin Ryan looked like a little lost puppy now, before he had even heard her sing a note, God only knew what she was going to look like when he told her *Sorry... don't give up the day job.*

Expelling an aggrieved sigh, he dragged his fingers impatiently through his mane of dark hair and stared at her.

'Okay,' he drawled, his tone painfully resigned, 'I'll give you ten minutes to show me what you can do.' *Or, more to the point, what you can't.* He couldn't pretend he was expecting very much.

Caitlin's heart beat double-time. *Okay, I can do this,* she told *herself. Singing is second nature to me.*

But her morale-boosting self-talk didn't seem to be having a great deal of effect as she nervously made her way across to the stage. The three young men already there ambled casually back to their instruments and she wondered how many singers they'd already auditioned—because frankly they weren't looking too impressed.

Registering the band's name on the large bass drum in front of the drum kit, and privately acknowledging that she'd never heard of it, she somehow made her lips shape a smile. The lead guitarist introduced himself first. Telling Caitlin that his name was Mike, he extended his hand to help her as she negotiated the final step of the wooden staircase that led onto the stage. He had an open, friendly face she noted, unlike *Captain Ahab* down there, who looked as if he'd just as soon as take a bite out of her rather than throw away a smile on someone who was clearly a time-waster.

Why, oh, why had she thought this was a good idea? Just because she loved to sing, it didn't mean that she had anywhere *near* enough talent to make it her career…

'By the way, I'm Rick. The man who told you to come back tomorrow is the head honcho. Aren't you going to take off your coat?'

At the foot of the stage the fair-haired man who'd persuaded his boss to give her a chance grinned up at her, with a teasing twinkle in his dancing hazel eyes that was in complete contrast to the reception Caitlin had received from his stony-faced colleague.

As his dark, brooding friend stayed ominously at the back of the hall she noticed he was staring back at her, as if to say, *Your performance is going to have to be exceptional if you're going to impress me.* He was regarding her as if he fully expected her to disappoint him. *Who was he anyway? Caitlin wondered?* He might be the man in charge of the auditions, but although he'd asked for her name he hadn't volunteered his own.

In answer to Rick's comment about removing her coat, she answered, 'I'd rather keep it on, if you don't mind. I'm feeling a little bit chilly.'

Her hand curved round the mike stand as if to anchor her to something solid. *Oh, why had she worn this stupid short skirt?* Because her friend Lia had told her she should make an effort to 'look nice' for the audition, that was why. Caitlin should have stuck to her preference of wearing jeans and a T-shirt.

Raising his voice so that she could hear him clearly, Rick asked, 'So what are you going to sing for us?'

Caitlin told him. It was a song that was regarded as a classic in the annals of rock culture. Although it had a driving, pulsing beat, there was also great passion and pathos in the lyrics and she loved it.

'Good song choice.'

She couldn't help colouring at the approval in his voice and turned her head towards the band so that he wouldn't see he'd unsettled her. 'Is that okay with you?' she asked them.

The blond bearded drummer, who'd introduced himself as Steve Bridges, answered her with a precise drumroll, and to Caitlin's right the stocky Scottish bass player, whose name was Keith Ferguson, played a couple of chords on his guitar.

'Let's rock and roll, then, shall we?' Rick gave her a mock salute. 'It's all yours, honey. Take it away.'

I can do this, Caitlin told herself dry-mouthed as she waited for the band to play her in.

For a couple of seconds she squeezed her eyes shut tight. If she wanted to stay strong she wouldn't glance at Mr Tall, Dark and Foreboding, lest one disapproving look from those strangely light blue eyes of his smothered the small vestige of courage she had left. But as the music struck up around her fear helpfully receded, replaced by her desire to sing.

She knew this particular number inside out. What she *wouldn't* admit to the present company was that she'd only sung it in the bath or in the privacy of her bedroom. *Oh, and once to Lia.* Her lack of experience would really freak them out if they knew about it before they heard her. Suppressing a suddenly uncharacteristic urge to grin, she listened for her cue, then opened her mouth and launched into the vocal.

Electricity shot through Jake's system with all the power of a lightning bolt. His stomach muscles clenched hard as excitement and shock suffused him. As he listened to the honeyed, sexy vocal emanating from the raven-haired beauty onstage he knew they'd struck gold. He didn't even have to let her finish the song to know it, but of course he would.

Caitlin's classy vocals melded with the rich, tight sound the band had worked so hard to attain as though they'd been made for each other. Her performance was stand-out amazing…knee-buckling.

Catching sight of the exchanged grins between the band members, he also saw Rick's silently mouthed *'Eureka'* as he turned round to give Jake the thumbs-up. There wasn't one girl Jake had heard sing in the past four days who came even remotely close to the talent of Caitlin Ryan. Hell...there wasn't one girl he'd heard sing in the past couple of *years* who was even in her league. The woman delivered a song as if she was born to it. *Damn.*

He moved his head in wonder as he watched her, her body moving in a naturally sexy sway to the beat of the music, her shapely legs drawing his appreciative gaze despite her strange insistence on keeping her coat on. With the right clothes and make-up this girl would be sit up and beg gorgeous. As good a singer as Marcie had been, she couldn't hold a candle to Caitlin Ryan in the looks department. He didn't wholly go along with the idea that a singer needed to be attractive, but good looks certainly didn't hurt in this business.

Suddenly his desire for sustenance at the local pub dissipated like snow in the desert. Jake was excited again. Enthused. When the mood was on him he could work twenty-four hours a day without a break if he wanted to, and he would willingly do so to get this band on the road again, expecting nothing less than the same commitment from everyone else.

As the last chords of the music died away Caitlin inhaled a relieved breath to steady herself. Then she reluctantly released the microphone.

Behind her, Steve Bridges blew an appreciative whistle. 'That was incredible. You absolutely killed it.'

Feeling her face grow warm at the compliment, she was taken aback when the two men who had been watching her vaulted onto the stage.

'What other bands have you been in?' Jake demanded.

Glancing back into his mesmerising eyes—eyes the colour of blue ice melting under steam—Caitlin's heart bungee-jumped to her toes. 'I—I haven't been in any other bands,' she admitted softly.

'You're kidding me.' Rick looked completely nonplussed.

Startled that he didn't believe her, she widened her eyes in surprise.

'I wouldn't pretend about something like that. The truth is I've only ever sung for my own amusement and because I'm compelled to. I just love music. I'm passionate about it.'

The rock-hard muscles in Jake's stomach compressed tightly. *He could tell she had passion...had it in spades, he thought.* That was the major difference between her and the instantly forgettable *wannabes* he'd recently auditioned.

'So you've never sung professionally before?' he queried.

'No. I haven't.' Her huge green eyes were absolutely guileless. Gazing back into their depths was like looking down to the bottom of a clear unsullied lake on a hot summer's day.

'So, what do you do to keep body and soul together?'

'You mean for a living?' Caitlin sighed. 'I'm a shop assistant. Remember I told you I had to stand in for the manager earlier today?'

'And where is the shop?'

'It's here in the village, of course.'

Jake was honestly stunned. They'd been auditioning girls from as far afield as Scotland, and this girl—this incredible find of theirs—came from the very village they were auditioning in. It was altogether ludicrous.

Laughing out loud, Rick slapped his leather-clad thigh. 'Well, if that doesn't beat it all! You mean for the past four days now we've been tearing our hair out trying to find a singer and you've been here all the time?'

'I only found out about the auditions when I saw the ad in the post office. I couldn't believe it. Nothing as exciting as that ever happens in the village. It seemed...' she flushed a little '...it seemed like a sign.' Tucking some silky strands of ebony hair behind an ear, Caitlin smiled self-consciously. 'Anyway…thanks for hearing me and giving me the chance to sing for you. Whatever happens, I really enjoyed it.'

She turned away to climb back down from the stage and leave, but was taken aback when Jake held up his hand, a distinctly puzzled crease straining his handsome brow.

'Where do you think you're going?'

'I've got to get back to work. I—I told you…we're stock-taking. I don't suppose we'll finish until late tonight.'

'Do you want to sing with this band or not?' he demanded, hardly able to believe what he was hearing.

'Do you mean…? Are you saying…?'

The stunned look on her face would be almost comical if Jake had a mind to laugh—which he absolutely *didn't*.

'On the strength of the performance we've just heard, I think I'd be a fool not to offer you the chance of singing with the band. I think we're all in agreement that you're just what we're looking for.'

Even though he directed a meaningful glance towards Rick and the others, Jake barely needed confirmation of his decision. Not when the final say categorically rested with him.

Eyes narrowing, he continued, 'But if we take you on you do realise that there's a hell of a lot of work ahead of you? You may be able to sing, Miss Ryan, but there's a lot to learn before we let you loose onstage in public. Have you honestly never sung professionally before?'

He didn't believe her. As exciting as the prospect of singing with the band was, Caitlin knew instinctively that if she accepted the job her relationship with this man was never going to be one made in heaven.

She nervously cleared her throat. 'I was in a school band from fifteen to eighteen, but I've done nothing since then. We only played local functions. Events like Christmas parties, special birthdays and anniversaries…stuff like that'

'And you were the lead singer?'

'No. That is…we all sang. There were six of us altogether. But I occasionally played piano and guitar.'

Rick's eyebrows flew up to his hairline. 'You're a musician as well?'

'Yes. That is, I read music and play a little. I practise whenever I can…at least on my guitar. I no longer have a piano.'

No wonder she knew instinctively exactly where to come in with the vocal, Jake mused. Only someone who was a competent musician or had a natural ear for music could pull that off without rehearsal.

He saw his astonishment reflected back at him when his glance collided with Rick's.

'Sweetheart, as far as I'm concerned there's not the slightest doubt in my mind that you're the right singer for this band.' The American smiled, his hand enthusiastically shaking Caitlin's. 'By the way, my full name is Rick Young— I'm Blue Sky's official dogsbody and general "helper-outer". That means I organise the gigs, make sure the band shows up on time, and most importantly collect the fee at the end of the show. The man standing beside you with the poker face is Jake Sorenson—well-known record producer and the band's manager. You must have heard of him? Anyway, he's going to make us all rich one day, like him. You can count on it. If anyone can work miracles round here, Jake can. He's been in the business so long he's probably due for a plaque in the Rock and Roll Hall of Fame.'

'Very funny.'

Jake didn't put out his hand for Caitlin to shake. *Right then he had the strangest feeling that if he did he wouldn't want to let it go.* If this venture was going to work at all then he needed to maintain the requisite professionalism at all times. The last thing he needed was to get personally involved with Little Miss Hole in her Stocking. The band had been through enough upheaval and disappointment with Marcie walking out. No… If they were going to work together then he was going to play strictly by the rules. He *had* to, no matter how irresistible the temptation. And if he should at any time forget that vow then all he had to do was remember the scandal that had near crushed him and killed his career.

Taking a sidelong glance at Rick, and seeing that his friend's avidly appreciative gaze was all but glued to Caitlin, as if only a madman would want to look anywhere else, Jake firmed his resolve. 'Strictly by the rules' went for Rick and the guys, too. And, by God, he'd make sure that they knew it.

As the band welcomed Caitlin he saw that their pleasure was absolutely sincere. He also saw how her lovely face lit up at their enthusiastic welcome, how a faint flush of pink stained her cheeks as she strove to handle it, and something told Jake she was definitely an innocent compared to the rest of them. *That too could be a sticking point, he reflected*...especially in the dog-eat-dog world that was the music business. But, that said, it made a refreshing change to meet someone with hope and enthusiasm in their eyes— someone who wasn't old and jaded before their time as he probably was...

'Come into my office, Miss Ryan,' he invited her. 'We need to talk in private.'

Vaulting off the stage, Jake strode to the end of the hall, the sound of his boot heels echoing loudly in his wake.

After eagerly helping Caitlin down from the stage, Rick hurried to catch up to his enigmatic boss. 'Hey, don't you want me there too?' he called.

Turning, Jake shook his head, a muscle flexing in the side of his hollowed cheek. 'Not at the moment, my friend. There'll be time enough to go over the timetable for rehearsals when we talk later. We'll have a group meeting tomorrow afternoon so that we can discuss everything. Right now I just want to have a private chat with Miss Ryan'

'Miss Ryan?' Rick frowned. 'What's wrong with Caitlin?'

Ignoring the comment, Jake turned and opened his office door.

Her trepidation mingling with excitement, Caitlin followed him. The whole experience felt strangely surreal to her. The office that Blue Sky's charismatic manager was using was a room not much bigger than a generously-sized broom cupboard, she saw. All it contained were two grey plastic chairs and an upturned orange box masquerading as a table. One small window allowed just a paltry glimpse of sky.

Moistening her lips, Caitlin sucked in a breath. Somehow being in such close proximity to Jake Sorenson was ten times more testing than any audition she could imagine. He had the kind of highly charged aura round him that would stir the senses of a blind woman, she mused nervously.

'Take a seat,' he instructed.

Feeling undeniably overwhelmed, she complied. When she sat, her knees unavoidably pressed up against the rough wood of the orange box as she strove to make herself more comfortable. Adjusting her coat as she waited for Jake to carry on speaking, she felt her anxiety definitely intensify.

'You've already told me that you have a job. I presume that's full-time?' Flipping open the black notebook on top of the box, he started writing inside it.

'That's right.'

'You said you work in a shop? What kind of shop?' Lifting his head, Jake pinned her to the seat with his pale blue eyes.

'It's a shop called Morgana,' she told him. 'It specialises in esoteric and personal development books, but we also sell things like incense, Native American jewellery, ambient music and crystals.'

And I love working there, she silently reflected. She shifted in the hard plastic chair. It would be a real wrench to leave that job, but what was the point in having a passion in life if you weren't planning on doing anything about it? Her friend Lia knew just how much Caitlin loved music, how she loved to sing. And then Caitlin had told her that she'd seen an ad in the post office

Versatile female singer aged twenty to thirty wanted to front established band specialising in soft rock.

Auditions were being held in St Joseph's church hall, in the very village where they lived, and Lia had encouraged her to go for it.

'It must be clear to you that if you want to sing with this band you can't work full-time in a shop as well?'

Jake didn't take his eyes off of her as he addressed Caitlin, and the blatant directness of his unsettling blue gaze made her feel as if someone had just curtailed her oxygen supply.

'Rehearsals start tomorrow afternoon and will continue every day after that for the next three weeks before the band performs in public. After that we'll be all over the country for an initial three-week tour. Are you ready to commit to such a schedule, Miss Ryan?'

'I hadn't really thought about much beyond the audition,' she confessed honestly, 'but I realise whoever gets the job will have to be prepared to do regular gigs and eventually tour. So, yes, I am ready to commit, Mr Sorenson. I've never wanted anything more.'

'And you know that means giving up your present job to do so?'

'Of course.'

Although she hadn't hesitated to answer in the affirmative Jake didn't miss the slightly perturbed frown between her elegant brows, and once again he had the distinct impression that Caitlin was a relative innocent when it came to the type of worldly experience that the rest of them had.

'Does that worry you?' he asked.

Lifting her chin, she was intent on holding his gaze and not shying away from it, he saw.

'I'd be a liar if I said it wasn't daunting to leave something I'm so familiar with for something much more challenging, but I want to rise to that challenge. Especially if it's going to help me realise my dream of becoming a professional singer. Besides…change is inevitable, isn't it? Nothing stays the same.'

'You don't have to make it sound like it's something to fear. There's many a singer who'd give their eye-teeth to have the opportunity I'm offering you. Blue Sky may have lost their lead vocalist but they're still an established band. Just before Marcie left they were invited to play on one of the top music shows on television.'

And the guys had been gutted when they'd had to cancel the engagement. It might have been the big break they'd been praying for…

'Please don't think that I'm ungrateful.'

Shifting self-consciously in her seat, Caitlin snagged her stocking on a splinter from the orange box. As she picked at it to free herself she blushed scarlet, because Jake's gaze was suddenly focused on her knee instead of on her face. The very air between them seemed to throb with heat and a disturbing prickle of perspiration slid worryingly down her spine.

'I think I'm still in shock,' she admitted, 'I didn't expect to get as far as this. I'm still trying to take it all in.'

'Well…' Reluctantly withdrawing his glance from her knee, Jake strove to remain businesslike. 'I'm not asking you to sign on the dotted line tonight. But that doesn't mean I'm giving you the chance to change your mind. When I've decided that I want something, Caitlin, I won't rest until I get it. So be here tomorrow at five. We'll be rehearsing until late in the evening. Do we have a deal?'

She bit down on her lip. 'Yes—yes, we do. But can I make it five-forty-five instead? I have to close the shop at five-thirty. I won't be any later. I can be here in just ten minutes if I drive.'

'Five-forty-five it is, then. And before you leave you'd

better give me your address and mobile phone number, just
in case.'

Caitlin gave him the information and watched warily as
Jake scribbled it down in his black notebook. Then he threw
down his pen and got to his feet. She followed suit, her heart
racing as he towered over her. She was five foot seven in
her bare feet, but his physical domination of the tiny space
seemed to make the already diminutive room even smaller.

Her fingers shaking, she fastened a couple of her coat
buttons and managed a tentative smile. 'I'll see you tomorrow then, Mr...?' She had a moment of panic because she'd
somehow forgotten his surname.

'You can call me Jake.'

To her utter surprise and secret delight a dimple appeared
as if by magic at the corner of his very sexy mouth. Caitlin's
insides knotted painfully.

'Right.'

'There's just one more thing before you go.'

'What's that?'

'I'd better explain one of the most important house rules,
and that is there's to be no fraternising after hours with members of the band—and I'm not talking about a few drinks
backstage after a gig. Am I making myself clear?'

Now Caitlin's face really *did* burn. She tried to look
anywhere but straight at Jake. If he seriously thought she
would—that she might— Of course he could have no idea
that she'd sworn off men for good, she realised. But after
what she'd been through with her ex-boyfriend Sean she'd
rather trek through the Sahara Desert with a fur coat on
than risk another soul-destroying relationship with a man...
however brief.

'All I want to do is sing. I'm not interested in anything
else. I can positively assure you of that.'

Jake couldn't help wondering why. He'd glimpsed pain
and fury in those pretty green eyes of hers just now, as if
even the suggestion that she might find herself attracted to

a member of the opposite sex was tantamount to contemplating suicide.

He sighed. 'Okay, then. There's just one other thing.'

'What's that?'

This time Caitlin's wary gaze met his in pure defiance, as though she dared him to transgress one more inch into her private life.

Jake ventured a teasing smile. 'I'd seriously think about investing in a new pair of stockings, if I were you'

'How did you know they were—?'

'How did I know that they were stockings and not tights?' He gave her a shameless grin. 'Put it down to long experience…' he drawled, pretty sure that if he told her he'd had a tantalising glimpse of her stocking-tops when she'd first sat down she'd exit so fast he wouldn't see her for dust. 'You can't beat the genuine article.'

'Is that so? Well, anyway…I didn't know you could tell.' With a disturbed frown Caitlin tried to remember to breathe. Sheer embarrassment made her babble. 'The trouble is I seem to have an unhappy knack of snagging them whenever I wear them. They're not really practical. I normally wear jeans.'

'Take it from me…' Jake's voice dropped down a discernible notch or two, making his tone arrestingly smoky '…stockings are better…'

CHAPTER TWO

THE DOORBELL JANGLED and the wind chimes that hung liberally from the lilac-painted ceiling tinkled prettily in the ensuing draught. As far as Caitlin knew, Nicky, their part-time help, was around somewhere, and should have registered the fact that they had customers, but she must have absented herself to go to the bathroom.

Sighing softly, she didn't look round, in the belief that the other girl would appear any minute now, and instead continued to scrub at the particularly stubborn patch of dirt she'd found on the lowest shelf of the temporarily emptied bookshelf. When the stain didn't respond to her increased scrubbing with a damp cloth Caitlin scratched at it with her fingernail, a spurt of annoyance shooting through her when she realised it was the horrid remains of someone's chewing gum.

Of all the... She was immediately affronted on Lia's behalf. How dared someone come into this beautiful space and foul it with chewing gum? Some people just didn't have any respect. Some people just—

'Hi, there.'

Caitlin froze at the sound of that smoky bass voice. Still tense, she turned her head and glanced up to meet Jake Sorenson's indisputably amused glance. Had it really been just a day since she'd last seen him? Was it possible she could have so easily forgotten how dangerously attractive the man was, or that his mere presence had the power to erase anything else from her mind?

Irritated by her purely female response to his tall, dark good looks, she realised she was gaping up at him. What was even worse, he'd caught her wearing an old and tatty pair of jeans that had shrunk in the wash and now adhered to her thighs like a second skin. Caitlin had opted to wear them because she knew she'd be undertaking some general cleaning that day and hadn't wanted to risk ruining any of her good clothes. What made things worse was that she'd also elected to don a favourite old red T-shirt that had also seen better days, and it clung where it didn't ought to cling, possibly inviting too much unwanted attention...like *now*, when Jake's disturbing light blue eyes were making a slow and deliberate inventory of her body.

Heat crawled up her spine...*sexual* heat. It completely undid her. Just what was he *doing* here? Couldn't he have telephoned if he'd needed to speak to her? He had an unfair advantage, taking her by surprise like this.

Leaving her cloth on the bookshelf, she abruptly turned and got to her feet. Long strands of glossy black hair escaped her loosely tied ponytail to drift down gently over her flushed cheeks, and there was a smudge of dust on her nose. She struggled to get her greeting past her lips.

'Hi. I'm sorry, but you've caught me at a rather awkward moment. I was...'

'Let me guess...stocktaking?' Jake drawled softly.

She swallowed hard. The man could read a technical pamphlet on assembling flat-pack furniture out loud and it would still make her hot. 'Cleaning. I was just cleaning. Stocktaking was yesterday.'

'It's nice to see such dedication to the task. You looked like you were giving it your all.' Smiling faintly, he glanced round him. 'Interesting shop,' he remarked, sliding his hands into the back pockets of his jeans and nodding to himself as his gaze made another leisurely reconnaissance.

The heady scent of sandalwood incense perfumed the air and Caitlin wondered for the first time ever if it wasn't just a tad overpowering. Why she should suddenly be concerned about such an inconsequential thing, she didn't know. All she knew was that she wanted Jake to get a good impression of her workplace and not judge it adversely.

Jake's interested glance narrowed as he examined some of the titles on the bookshelves either side of the ones Caitlin had been cleaning. He glimpsed. *Living Your Destiny* and other esoteric titles and permitted himself a smile. He'd known many hippies in his time, who had loved this kind of stuff. He looked up. From the painted ceiling dangled a myriad of wind chimes and crystals, and the music of some Native American drums pulsed gently. But, as eye-catching and diverting as the room furnishings were, he had no trouble bringing his gaze straight back to Caitlin.

He hadn't forgotten how pretty she was, and he was certain that the shape that had been intriguingly hidden behind her coat yesterday would be equally arresting…especially as he'd already been treated to the sight of her long slim legs in those tantalising black stockings. But nothing had quite prepared him for the mouth-wateringly feminine curves that he was looking at now.

Her scarlet T-shirt was at least one size smaller than she needed and it clung sexily to her voluptuous breasts, with the light stretchy fabric hugging her delectable shape like a second skin. Hell, he was on fire—uncharacteristically caught off-guard by his acute reaction to the green-eyed temptress in front of him. There was a tense knot in the pit of his stomach as he tried to tamp down the forceful desire that gripped him.

As he stared helplessly he registered the distinct outline of Caitlin's nipples beneath her bra—and was it his fevered imagination or had they just puckered a little tighter? He'd already been treated to the tempting sight of her delightful derriere as she'd crouched down, cleaning the bookshelf, and God help him, why did he have the distinct feeling that Christmas had arrived early? Because it wasn't just Caitlin's vocal talent that would put Blue Sky on the map. The woman's stunning beauty would put some serious icing on the Christmas cake too.

'My friend Lia owns the shop.'

Folding her arms protectively across her chest, because she'd mortifyingly caught Jake's gaze straying there, Caitlin silently berated herself for wearing that particular shirt today of all days. But then how was she to have known that Jake would pay an impromptu visit?

'As I told you, she's at the dental hospital today, otherwise I'd introduce you.' Her gaze automatically gravitated to the counter, missing the familiar sight of a diminutive slim blonde with elfin features and soft brown eyes.

Nicky must be taking a bathroom break. Caitlin couldn't help wishing that the girl's timing had been better. Just my luck, she thought. If Nicky had been around she could have somehow diverted Jake's attention. But he surely hadn't visited the shop to browse...

'Anyway, what can I do for you?' she asked.

Jake stared at her in bemusement. *You wouldn't believe how creative I could get about that,* he thought, and then gave himself a harsh mental shake. Where were his brains, for goodness' sake? He had a perfectly legitimate reason for seeking out their new vocalist and yet he was standing there gawping at her like some horny teenager hoping to get laid. The realisation was sobering.

'About the rehearsals this afternoon,' he started, 'I just wanted to let you know that we'll be working quite late tonight—perhaps into the early hours of the morning. If you have a boyfriend I hope he's the understanding type. If not, we're all in trouble.'

'There's no boyfriend.'

'Good.'

Caitlin frowned. Rubbing her hands briefly up and down her bare arms, she glanced back into Jake's arresting blue gaze. The man had the kind of reined-in sexuality and physicality that couldn't help but put her on her guard. It didn't help matters that he had a 'bad boy' smile that was surely reserved for a woman's wildest fantasy...*if* she was in the market for such a fantasy—which she most definitely wasn't.

Still, the hard honed body outlined by his black T-shirt, jeans and fashionably battered leather jacket would surely be a thing of beauty without clothes. There was not so much as a hint of surplus flesh on that taut, streamlined physique. The man clearly kept himself in good shape. She couldn't prevent the small shiver of appreciation that ran up her spine. But it wasn't just the commanding, easy-on-the-eye physique that made Caitlin so intimately aware of him. Something told her that Jake Sorenson didn't take any prisoners. When he told her that they would be working late tonight she was certain he meant it in the fullest sense of the word.

What if I've made a terrible mistake? she fretted. *It's the thing I want to do more than anything else in the world, but what if I'm really not cut out to be a singer in a band?*

Her mind slipped into panic mode, as it was apt to do when she was hit by a sudden attack of self-doubt.

He must have read her mind just then. 'Don't look so terrified,' he cautioned, amusement lurking in the steamy blue depths of his mesmerising eyes. 'I promise not to drive you too hard on your first night. But after that I'm afraid you'll just have to roll with the punches like everybody else. Anyone who wants to pursue a dream has to make sacrifices, and the music business is a hard game, Caitlin. It's notoriously competitive and cut-throat, and that's an almost conservative description. If you want to be a success in this game you have to grow a fairly thick skin. Blue Sky have played all over the country in the past two years, trying to establish themselves, and they've gained a loyal following. When their lead singer Marcie walked out it was a huge shock. More than that it was a betrayal. But I owe it to the rest of the band to make good on my promise to take them to the top—and, trust me, I'm going to do exactly that. Failure is just not an option in my book. Do you understand what I'm saying?'

Caitlin did. *Signing up for commando training with the SAS would probably be easier.* She tried for a smile but couldn't help the nervous little quiver that hijacked her lips instead. Was the man always so serious, she wondered?

'I'll try my best not to let you down...Jake.' She added his name because she reasoned she should start being less formal, and couldn't help savouring the taste of it on her tongue— like an enticing new flavour she'd never sampled before.

He scowled.

'That's not good enough. Say, *I won't let you down, Jake.* Not, *I'll try.*'

Flustered, Caitlin pushed a stray strand of hair away from her suddenly burning cheek. 'I *won't* let you down, Jake.'

'That's better. Now, come here.'

Before she'd gleaned what he intended he firmly drew her towards himthen gently erased the smudge of dust she'd inadvertently acquired on her nose. Her senses were immediately bombarded by the warm sexy tang of leather mixing provocatively with the alluring masculine scent of the man himself.

If someone could bottle it, they'd make a fortune, Caitlin thought. She felt more than a little off-centre as she stepped away, especially when she saw that he was smiling. A deep, sensual tug registered low in her belly.

'Thanks. I'm probably covered in dust and looking a right mess, aren't I?' she remarked nervously.

The words were out before she could check them. She could have kicked herself, because now Jake would think she was fishing for a compliment—which was absurd when she did honestly believe she must resemble something the cat had dragged in.

But with a charismatic quirk at a corner of his lips Jake elected not to comment. Instead he walked to the door, opened it and gave her a brief salute. 'I'll see you tonight. Five-forty-five. Don't be late.'

As he stepped out onto the pavement Caitlin had a distinct sense of being dismissed. More to the point, she felt bereft, as if he'd somehow taken a part of her with him. The bell jangled as the door swung back on its hinges and she released a long slow breath, as though she'd been holding on to it for nothing less than a lifetime.

The realisation that she was late, even though she had a perfectly legitimate reason, made Caitlin furious with herself. Parking her car on the gravel drive that led up to the sombre-looking Victorian church hall, she bit back a ripe curse, fumbling to organise her car keys and purse as she shut the car door behind her. To add insult to injury, a light rain had started to fall.

She glanced down at her watch and her anxious gaze once more registered the time. *Six-fifteen...* She wasn't just late—she was *very* late. But how was she to have known that a customer would walk in the door at exactly a minute before five-thirty? She could hardly turn the girl away—especially when she'd tearfully told Caitlin that she'd just broken up with her boyfriend and someone had recommended she get some rose quartz to help her.

Lia had often teased her friend that she was a magnet for the heartsick, but Caitlin's naturally compassionate nature wouldn't allow her to stand back and do nothing when someone was hurting. When push came to shove, though, however she explained her tardiness to Jake Sorenson something told her it wasn't going to cut any ice.

Summoning every scrap of courage she could muster, she pushed open the creaky wooden door that led into the porch, wrinkling her nose at the pall of mustiness and damp that clung to the air, her heart bumping against her ribs at the sound of instruments tuning up.

Behind the door that led into the cavernous hall Jake was testing the microphone in the familiar time-honoured way of performers the world over: '*One two, one two...*'

Murmuring a briefly fervent prayer, Caitlin pushed open the door. The overhead lights were dimmed, she noticed, and the three members of the band on stage continued to play as Rick Young melted out of the shadows to position himself in front of her. Despite his serious expression, at least his hazel eyes were twinkling, she saw.

'You're late, pretty lady. Not a good start, just thought I'd warn you.'

He jerked his chin towards Jake as Blue Sky's enigmatic manager jumped off the stage, his long jeans-clad legs carrying him purposefully towards Caitlin. It didn't take a genius to deduce that he wasn't happy. *Blast!*

Her chilled fingers curled over the car keys in her pocket and held them tight. It wasn't as if she was late deliberately. She honestly wanted to take this amazing opportunity they were offering her. But right now, judging by the fierce scowl on Jake's handsome face, it might just be about to be taken away from her.

'I'm sorry I'm late. I just—'

'What was the last thing I said to you?' he barked.

Startled, Caitlin glanced across at Rick. His expression conveyed that he'd witnessed similar scenarios too many times before to be at all perturbed.

'Don't be late?' she ventured, her teeth anxiously clamping down on her lip.

'And didn't I also tell you to be here at five-forty-five? It's now twenty past six. You're thirty-five minutes late. That's not acceptable, Miss Ryan. It's not acceptable at all.'

Jake was shifting restlessly from one black-booted foot to the other, a muscle ominously flinching in the side of his lean, unshaven jaw. Caitlin didn't dare quip that his watch must be fast, even though it clearly *was*. The fact that he was unshaven made him look edgy and dangerous—as if anything could happen and probably would.

'A customer came into the shop just as I was getting

ready to leave—' the words came out in a heated rush as she gripped even more tightly onto her car keys.

'Couldn't you have turned whoever it was away and told them to come back tomorrow?' he snapped.

Affronted, Caitlin widened her eyes.

'I *never* turn customers away. People don't just come into our shop to buy things, Mr Sorenson. Many of them come in for healing of one kind or another. The girl that I saw was distraught. She'd just broken up with her long-term boyfriend and was looking for something that might help ease her distress. I'm not so cold-hearted that I would tell her in her hour of need to come back tomorrow.'

Jake was so taken aback by this answer that the red mist of anger that had threatened when Caitlin had walked in late dissipated like ice beneath the sun. Sucking in his cheeks, he blew out a long, slow breath, shaking his head and taking a moment to compose himself. *I must be losing my grip*, he thought irritably.

Caitlin proffered a hesitant smile. Jake's bemused glance collided with hers just as one corner of her pretty mouth nudged a very sexy dimple. Something hitched in his heart... not to mention below his navel.

'Well, we've wasted enough time as it is,' he growled. 'Take off your coat and get yourself up on stage. We've got a hell of a lot to get through tonight and we may well be here until breakfast—so be warned.'

After making her apologies to the other band members, seeing that Jake's attention had suddenly been claimed by Rick, Caitlin fell into animated conversation with them about music. Did they write all their own songs? Did they ever do any covers? And, finally, did they have a playlist for tonight's rehearsals that she could look at?

The young men were only too pleased to answer her questions, interspersing their answers with jokes and anecdotes and generally going out of their way to help put her at ease. Mike Casey, the lead guitarist, with his tousled dark hair and rather serious brown eyes, explained that he added the harmonies to several of the songs and he and Caitlin would need to spend some time together working on them. Then he told her that he and the others had rented a house in the village for the duration of their stay and she'd be more than welcome to come over and work on them there.

'Caitlin?'

She spun round at the sound of her name, folding her arms across the blue chambray man's shirt that she'd thrown over the too-revealing red T-shirt she'd been wearing earlier. The long shirt-tails skimmed her bottom in her tight jeans and helped her feel a little less vulnerable than she had done in the shop, when Jake's toe-curling glance had all but consumed her with its frank and hungry intensity.

She was staring into the same hauntingly blue depths now as he looked up at her from the foot of the stage. Her mouth dried. He handed her a sheet of paper with music and lyrics on. Accepting it without comment, she let her gaze fall eagerly on the title. It was another great rock standard that she knew by heart.

The lyrics were passionate and heart-rending, and she'd sung it with genuine feeling when she'd first learned it because she'd empathised with the sentiment of the song only too well. It was about a girl whose dreams had been cruelly shattered when the man she loved had used her and illtreated her and had consequently robbed her of every bit of self-confidence she had...

But now... Her glance quickly perused the musical arrangement and her heart skipped a nervous beat, because the time had come for her to really prove to both the band and their enigmatic manager that she could deliver what they hoped she could. It was one thing to conquer her fear of an audition—quite another to front a band for the first time ever and do it well. This was where things started to get serious.

'You know the tune? We can choose something more contemporary if you prefer?'

Jake's blue eyes honed in on the roomy chambray shirt Caitlin had donned over the sexy red T-shirt and once again he sensed that she wasn't at all at ease with her body. *Why else had she covered up?* And how would she cope when she had to perform on stage in front of a crowd he wondered? Would she be self-conscious then?

She was a naturally beautiful woman, and the sensual aura she exuded when she walked into a room was a killer. It was a given that her looks would be a big asset to the band, and he didn't want her to try and hide that sensational body behind oversized clothing. Still, there was plenty of time for that particular discussion. Right now Caitlin had to prove to them that she was a worthy replacement for Marcie.

'The song is fine' she told him. 'I know it well.'

'Good. Take it away, guys.'

As the band started to play the introduction Caitlin listened carefully, curving her hands round the microphone stand in readiness and staring towards the back of the hall rather than at Jake. Her body was tense as a sprinter's at the start of the most important race of her life, but she didn't need to glance at the lyrics as she waited for her cue to come in. The words were etched on her soul.

There was no need for her to imagine that she was the woman she was singing about because she *was*. She'd been used, hurt and scorned by a man she'd once loved and trusted, and the devastating experience had taught her to keep her guard up. Adversity had taught her a huge lesson and, hard as it was, it had helped her to grow stronger.

I'll put steel round my heart that your poison arrows can't dent
And I'll be the phoenix rising that you never saw coming...

Those were the lyrics.

Suddenly her eyes flew open and Caitlin's glance fell on

Jake. He was attired from head to toe in black, and his concentrated expression was utterly serious as he watched her performance. Minutes later, when she came to the end of the song, she was glad, because she desperately needed to suck in a steadying breath. Her heart was thumping hard at the painful memories the words had evoked. *Yet, meeting Jake's gaze once again, she didn't immediately withdraw when it hit her that he had seriously begun to fascinate her.*

It was probably just hormones, she thought irritably. She certainly wasn't looking to take things further than a working relationship. Apart from it being against the rules, she wasn't looking for a man. Just like in the song, Caitlin had had the relationship from *hell* with one particular man and it had nearly destroyed her. She certainly wasn't going to entertain the idea of being with someone who could twist her insides into knots merely by looking at her.

'Not bad,' he said grudgingly.

Her fervent hope had been that she'd done much better than just 'not bad', and Caitlin's heart plummeted. Still, Jake was the boss, and she wasn't there simply in search of praise. Her ambition was to earn her living as a bona fide singer—never to be dependent on anyone either for love, self-esteem or security.

That was why seeing the ad for the auditions had excited her. It really had seemed like a sign that she should step up to the plate and start to fulfil her destiny. Staying at the shop and 'playing safe' just didn't feel like the right option any more. Her family had moved on and so should she. *It wasn't the possibility of fame that interested her...far from it.* Her passion was the music itself—the potential to experience joy in doing what she loved to do and to share it with anyone who cared to listen.

So she would bow to the man's far greater experience in such matters and give her all to improve. She prayed her efforts would be enough.

'Wow! Honey, you'll never be poor with a voice like that,' Rick told her as he went to stand next to his friend.

The contrast between the two men was striking. Rick's longish tousled hair was tinted a sun-kissed blond, while Jake's was a dark chestnut-brown, and their physiques were markedly different too. Jake was broad-shouldered and lean, his body supremely fit and toned, while Rick was shorter and more muscular. But, whatever the contrast in appearance, Caitlin sensed the two men were firm friends. There was a definite camaraderie between them that suggested their association had been born out of knowing each other for a very long time.

'She was fantastic,' Rick commented, turning towards Jake. 'I felt every ounce of emotion she put into the song… she made it her own.'

'That may be true,' Jake responded, his cool glance deliberately sliding away from Caitlin's. 'But it won't belong to her until she knows it intimately, inside and out. Let's do it again, guys. Then you can do some of your own material.'

It was three hours later when Caitlin was finally able to take a breather. Perched on the edge of the stage, with her long slender legs dangling over the side, she was attempting to eat her portion of the Chinese take-away that Rick had ordered. Her throat ached, her head throbbed and she could have fallen asleep standing up.

The band's charismatic manager hadn't let up for one minute in his efforts to get the best out of her vocal performance and she felt as if she'd done twelve rounds with a prize fighter. Whilst she was perfectly aware that singing was a very physical occupation, even if a person was blessed with a good voice, nothing could have prepared Caitlin for the sheer effort that Jake demanded.

During the past three hours she'd survived admonition after admonition to, 'Try again!' 'Put your heart into it, woman!' 'Hold back a little on that note…drop down a

key…' *'Damn it, Caitlin! You're just not trying hard enough!'*
Now she could barely summon up the energy to eat, despite
the fact that the shrimp chop suey and bamboo shoots with
Chinese mushrooms looked and smelled delicious.

'Not hungry?'

Her tired glance fell on Jake's long jeans-clad legs as he
dropped down beside her. Her heart skipped a beat. Lifting
her gaze, she looked up into the hauntingly misty depths of
his soulful blue eyes. It struck her as unfair that a man should
possess such enviably long black lashes, but then she mused
that Jake must have been at the head of the line when God
was dishing out extraordinary good looks…not to mention
sheer animal magnetism.

Caitlin sucked in a less than steady breath when the
scent of his cologne forged another assault on her belea-
guered senses. In answer to his question, she responded, 'I
thought I was.' Shrugging, she put her carton of food aside
and touched a paper napkin delicately to her lips. 'I only
had a sandwich at lunchtime…it wasn't very nice either.'

'You must have known this wasn't going to be easy. Still
sure you want to go through with it?' Jake challenged. 'You
need more than just talent in this game, Caitlin. You need
equal measures of grit and stamina too.'

'I can summon up plenty of grit and stamina when I need
it. Just try me.'

A flash of defiance lit up her defensive green eyes and
Jake chuckled softly. She'd freed her lustrous long hair from
its ponytail and now it flowed down her back like shining
black silk. Examining it more closely, he detected flashes
of mahogany within the darker strands. His fingers were
itching to touch it and he closed his hands into fists to stop
himself from reaching out to do just that.

'It's obviously going to take me a little while to learn all
the new songs,' she breathed, 'but I'll take a copy of the music
and lyrics home with me and practise them on my guitar.'

Jake had almost forgotten that Caitlin was a guitarist as

well. How good he didn't yet know, but judging by her vocal talent he guessed it wouldn't be far behind.

'Good move,' he commented, 'but the first thing you're going to have to do is to hand in your notice at the shop. There's no way you can have a full-time job there outside of singing with the band. In just three weeks' time we'll be on the road and you'll have to kiss this sleepy little village goodbye.'

The words sounded so *final* that Caitlin couldn't help shivering. But she immediately reminded herself that the most amazing opportunity had come her way, and she should take it with open arms and think herself blessed. No one got anywhere in life without taking risks. God knew she should have absorbed that fact by now, with all the New Age reading she'd done since working for Lia.

She'd lived in the village for most of her life, having moved from London with her family when she was just a toddler. When her parents had decided to join her brother Phil and his wife in California three years ago Caitlin had opted to stay put. She wasn't ready to leave the country, she'd argued. There was still a lot to experience living in the UK.

But most of all she'd stayed because she'd needed time to forge her own identity—the chance to bring her own dreams into fruition, not just tag along on someone else's. *She'd even needed to make colossal mistakes, like her relationship with Sean.* None of those things would have been possible surrounded by her well-meaning but highly controlling family.

She swallowed hard.

'So…does that mean you're offering me a full-time position with the band?' she asked.

Her stomach churned as she waited for Jake's reply.

'Looks that way doesn't it?' He smiled. Then, agile as a cat, he leapt to his feet and crossed the stage to join Rick and the others.

CHAPTER THREE

'WE'RE ALL GOING back to the Pilgrim's Inn for a few drinks—want to join us?'

Mike Casey stood waiting as Caitlin shrugged into her raincoat. Everyone else was outside. Steve and Keith were loading the van with the equipment and Jake and Rick were deep in discussion. Rick had extended the same invitation to her earlier, and Caitlin had told him she'd think about it. But the very idea of going into that particular pub again, after what had happened between her and Sean on her last visit, made her feel faintly ill.

Sean had been so bad that night—out of his head on a cocktail of drink and drugs—and she'd feared the worst. She had been right to. The cruel words and jibes that he'd taunted her with had just got worse and worse as the evening progressed. . *The sharpest knife couldn't have cut her more deeply.* Add to that the humiliation of his verbal attack being witnessed by a pub full of people before the landlord threw him out—well, it had been enough to make her want to give the place a wide berth for ever.

Lifting her gaze to Mike's, she said, 'It's kind of you to ask me, but I think I'll have to say no. It's already quite late.'

Stealing a quick glance at her watch, she saw that it was ten-thirty-five, and they'd been rehearsing since three o'clock that afternoon. Her throat was parched and her body ached from the sheer effort that Jake had demanded. The man apparently had endless reserves of energy that made

Caitlin feel as if she was the slowest runner on the track in comparison. No. She'd much prefer to go home, shower, get into her pyjamas and put her feet up with a glass of wine and a bowl of crisps at her elbow.

'You call ten-thirty in the evening *late*? We're talking Saturday night, here. Don't tell me the whole village goes to bed early?' Mike's dark eyebrows flew up to the tips of his tousled fringe. 'You must have led a sheltered life, if that's normal for you.'

At his disbelieving grin, Caitlin conceded a shy smile. 'You must think I'm pretty boring, right? No way could I ever claim to be a typical rock chick, that's for sure. But I realise my early nights will have to come to an end when the band goes on the road.'

'You two ready?' Rick appeared at the door, his hazel eyes appraising Caitlin and Mike with interest. 'I have to lock up. Caitlin? Jake would like a word.'

What now? ow? Caitlin groaned inwardly at the prospect.

Jake hadn't lied when he'd said he would go easy with her on the first night but that after that she'd have to roll with punches like everyone else. He'd been harder on her than on any of the guys in the band. Maybe that was because they already knew what was required and she didn't? But somehow Caitlin didn't think that was the only reason Jake had been yelling at her all night.

Maybe he didn't like her. Maybe he was already regretting taking her on due to her lack of experience. She could speculate until night turned into day but she'd be none the wiser until they had a conversation.

Wearing his familiar black leather jacket over a sweatshirt and jeans, Jake was leaning against his Jeep. He straightened as Caitlin walked towards him, and even at the distance that separated them she sensed an undeniable magnetic charge that put her on her guard. It had started to rain, and the sound of the other band members' voices floated on the air as they huddled round the big white transit van they transported their equipment in.

As Jake continued to hold her gaze Caitlin sensed something register low in her belly—*a combination of fear, apprehension and irrefutable sexual attraction.* She didn't know whether to smile or run.

A fierce gust of wind just then almost tore her open raincoat from her shoulders, revealing her curvaceous figure in perhaps more detail than she wanted him to see. She felt alternately hot and cold all over as her boots crunched across the gravel.

'Rick said you wanted to speak to me?' She was slightly breathless as she presented herself, her long black hair lashing across her face in the wind and rain.

Straight away Jake noticed Caitlin shiver in her insubstantial raincoat. *He knew a way to warm her up.* Another place, another time, he might have given into such an urge. God knew Caitlin Ryan had been testing all his powers of self-control from the very first moment he'd set eyes on her.

'So, are you going to join us for a drink or what?' he asked tersely.

'That's what you wanted to talk to me about?'

Catching the ends of her raincoat belt, she twisted it tightly round her waist. In vain she tried to shove her long hair out of her eyes and noticed her hands were trembling. *What was it about this man that could unravel her so easily?*

'I already told Mike that I wasn't coming. I'm going home to get an early night.' she said. 'Don't worry I'll make sure I'm here at three o'clock on the dot for rehearsals tomorrow.'

'I want you to come for a drink.'

The pupils of Jake's eyes had turned unsettlingly dark… so dark that there was just the palest blue circle ringed round them.

'It's a good opportunity for us to get to know each other. Tomorrow's Sunday. You can have a lie-in.'

Caitlin could hardly argue with his reasoning, even if her

heart *was* fluttering madly at the very idea of spending the rest of the evening in the company of the charismatic band manager. But there was also the not exactly small matter of her showing up at the Pilgrim's Inn. There was always a small influx of visitors from outside the village, but generally customers were mostly a local crowd, and there were bound to be people there who remembered how Sean had humiliated her.

'I—I'd rather not come, if you don't mind.'

'The invitation was an order, not a choice. You're going to have to get used to late nights if you're going to sing with this band. Get in the car. You can ride with me and Rick'

So that was how Caitlin found herself squeezed into a worn red velvet corner seat in the pub, with Rick on one side and Jake on the other, as the band members stood round the cosy fire in the iron grate, hogging the heat and nursing their pints of beer.

From the jukebox Sting's voice boomed out: something about not standing so close... *Caitlin could easily have echoed the sentiment.* Rick had hung her raincoat over the back of a chair but she wasn't bereft of warmth—not when Jake's hard-muscled thigh was pressed against hers. A full-on radiator couldn't have made her hotter. Every time he shifted even slightly the renewed contact made Caitlin's heart miss a beat.

'So tell me, Cait. What music do you like to listen to?'

Rick had been shortening her name ever since they'd arrived at the pub and she tried not to flinch, because her ex, Sean, had always called her that. Her gaze anxiously swept the room. There were several groups of young people seated around the tables, clearly enjoying themselves. Thankfully nobody had paid her any particular attention. Behind the bar two barmaids were busily serving customers, and one of them, a voluptuous blonde named Tina Stevens, was wearing a neckline so low that if she wasn't careful she'd be arrested for indecency.

Bringing her attention back to Rick, Caitlin answered. 'Oh, I have such a wide taste you wouldn't believe it. If I had to sum it up I'd say I love music with a good beat and great songs with good lyrics. How about you? What do you enjoy listening to?'

Shrugging, Rick took a sip of his beer then put it carefully back down on the cork beer mat. 'My taste is very similar to yours, honey. It's clear that you and I have a lot in common, a *hell* of a lot in common, in fact.'

'That's the beer talking,' Jake observed wryly.

The gravelled intonation of his deep voice made all the hairs stand up at the back of Caitlin's neck. *Was it her imagination or had his thigh moved even closer to hers?*

'He's just trying to get into your good books.'

'That's unfair. A man like me doesn't have to *try* to get into any woman's good books. They naturally gravitate towards me. I'm gifted like that. Talking of which…'

Suddenly getting to his feet, Rick carefully eased his way round the table so as not to dislodge their drinks. Caitlin saw that his avid glance was focused determinedly on a smiling Tina Stevens behind the bar, who at that very moment was leaning dangerously across the counter in her figure-hugging red top, chatting to yet another appreciative male customer.

'Excuse me, guys, but I can see a maiden's honour is at stake if I don't go and rescue her…' Rick headed purposefully towards the bar.

Breathing out a relieved sigh, Caitlin was glad to have a little more room to manoeuvre, but she was still dizzy at the thought of having to deal with Jake on her own. As discreetly as she was able, she moved her leg away from the hot press of his jean-clad thigh.

'She'll have him for breakfast,' he said, and grinned.

The shock of suddenly meeting his steamy blue glance at such close quarters trapped Caitlin's breath somewhere between her throat and her mouth. She found herself a little too intimately aware of the faint shadow of beard across his top lip and jaw, his long straight nose and the sexy indentation in his sculpted chin. Most of all she was aware of the provocative message his hypnotic blue gaze seemed to be conveying to her. It was indisputably sexual. And it made every muscle in her body tighten and clench.

The whole room diminished down to just that look.

'He looks like he can take care of himself,' she murmured, hardly aware of moving her lips.

'So...' Taking a leisurely sip of his beer and studying her at the same time, Jake asked casually, 'Why no boyfriend?'

Hypnotised by the long fingers that curled round his glass, Caitlin found herself envying it his touch, wondering what it would be like to feel those same long fingers intimately touching *her*. The very notion made her *burn*, and she took a hurried sip of her dry white wine, deliberately focusing her gaze on the drink instead of him.

'I didn't know it was compulsory.'

'Did I imply it was?'

She didn't answer. Thinking about Sean and how she had let him come *that* close to wrecking her life was not something she wanted to revisit...certainly not in casual conversation.

The flash of pain he witnessed in Caitlin's eyes just then took Jake by surprise. As defensive as she undoubtedly was, she hadn't been quick enough to hide it. There were also faint lines of hurt round her mouth that betrayed her. *Clearly she had let someone get too close and got herself burned in the process.*

Even though he'd experienced a similar painful scenario in a relationship, something inside him said he should be careful not to let empathy lower his defences. Relationships by their nature were always going to be challenging, no matter what the situation. But Jake wasn't such a bastard that he couldn't find it in him to be concerned.

'So, what happened?'

'What do you mean?'

'You got hurt by a man,' he said thoughtfully. 'Who was he?'

'Do you mind if we don't talk about this?'

Jake's question was definitely too close for comfort. Taking another sip of wine, she felt her cheeks burn as she sensed the alcohol take effect.

'We're going to be spending a lot of time together over the next few weeks—the next few months, even. Things are bound to come out. Why not tell me now and get it over with?'

Inadvertently glancing down at her purple T-shirt, at the scooped neckline that revealed a tantalising glimpse of her cleavage, Jake felt the muscles in the pit of his belly clench. He shifted in his seat.

'That might be the case, but my personal life is not up for discussion. Please don't press me on this.'

There was a tremulous hitch in her voice that made Jake feel like the most insensitive oaf on earth. On impulse, he reached across and covered her hand with his own—even if he *did* risk going up in flames at the contact.

'I'm sorry...' he murmured.

Caitlin didn't know whether he meant he was sorry for putting pressure on her or whether he was sorry for what he guessed might have happened in her relationship. *Either way, she didn't welcome his sympathy.* It was easier to deal with his irritation. At least it stopped her feeling sorry for herself. In any case, she'd done enough wallowing in despair to last a lifetime.

But it was impossible not to stare down at the strong, capable hand covering hers. As she did so, she examined the unique silver and jet ring that he wore. It comprised two black stones in a figure of eight setting and didn't detract from his masculinity one iota... In fact it *enhanced* it. She found herself strangely reluctant to extricate herself.

Speaking her thoughts out loud, she commented, 'That's a beautiful ring.'

'Yes, it is. It was a gift.'

He probably should have got rid of the thing, come to think of it, because it certainly wasn't for sentimental reasons that he still wore it. But Jake wasn't about to tell Caitlin that the jewellery had been given to him by his ex-wife Jodie a year and a day after they were married and six months before they divorced.

It suddenly occurred to him to wonder if she'd read the sordid little story of their break-up in the newspapers at the time. But, as she hadn't even indicated that she knew who he was when they'd first met, Jake took refuge in the thought that perhaps the scandal had somehow passed her by.

Withdrawing his hand abruptly from hers, he glanced across the now slowly emptying pub at Rick, who was still engaged in conversation with the buxom Tina Stevens. There was no sign of the blonde's previous admirer, Jake saw.

Turning back to Caitlin, he asked, 'Have you had enough?' His glance fell on her barely drunk glass of wine.

'Is that a hint you want to leave?'

'I think I should take you home. You look done in.'

'You don't need to take me. I'm quite capable—'

'Why don't you just put your coat on?'

Outside the wind was fierce as Caitlin walked along the deserted pavement with Jake. He walked with eyes front, one hand jammed into the back pocket of his jeans, his handsome profile ominously unsmiling as his dark hair blew across his face.

'How far do you live from here?' he asked, 'We can take my car if you're tired. I've barely drunk anything at all.'

'I'm only ten minutes up the road and I prefer to walk. But I don't expect you to walk with me.'

Caitlin couldn't help feeling tense. It was near impossible to guess what he was thinking or feeling. The man was a law unto himself. And the tension between them hadn't eased one iota. If anything it was *worse*.

'So, how do you feel about the way things are going?'

Taking her by surprise, Jake turned his head to examine her as they walked. It took a few seconds for her to get her thoughts together.

'You mean the rehearsals? I think they're going well. I mean, I know I've still got a lot to learn, but as well as learning the songs when I'm with the band I'm working on them at home whenever I get the time.'

She tucked her flying hair behind her ear and tried to relax, but it was hard when her companion's enigmatic expression hardly revealed what he might be feeling.

He sighed. 'You're doing just fine, Caitlin. I have no doubt that you're the perfect singer for Blue Sky. I'm you're got a great voice, you're beautiful and sexy…you're the whole package. But even great talent can't make it work on its own. Blue Sky isn't some five-minute wonder, like some of these manufactured bands that litter the charts. A lot of those bands are the product of slick marketing, purely designed to make money. They're not about real, dedicated musicians who get together because they're passionate about music. I told you it wasn't going to be easy. If anything, it's going to get harder. There's still a lot of work ahead before we start touring, and then the pressure really will be on. I suppose I just want to know whether your commitment is total, or whether you wouldn't prefer staying here in the village, working in your little book store? Don't get me wrong—I can see how that must have its appeal for a girl like you.'

'What do you mean, a girl like me?' Already bristling at what she perceived as Jake's patronising tone, Caitlin glared at him in the lamplight. 'You don't even *know* me.'

Raising a dark eyebrow, he smiled. 'I know you like to pretend you're tougher than you look, that you can handle anything I throw at you, but—'

'Stop right there!' Her hackles were really up now. '*Pretend* I'm tough? Do you think I'm such a wilting flower I'll break at the first sign of pressure? For your information, I survived two years of hell with a man who was a drug ad-

dict and alcoholic who took me for every penny I had. I even
had to sell my piano, and it was my dearest possession. As
well as that I lost my home, my car and my dignity. I lost it
all just to pay for his drug habit. Yes, I was a fool—but one
day I woke up and found the strength to tell him enough was
enough. Then I picked up the broken pieces of what was left
of my life and started over. I've survived hardship and pain
and I'm all the stronger for it—so don't you dare tell me I
pretend I'm tough!'

She paused to take a breath.

'As for wanting to be in the band—singing *is* and always
was my greatest passion and I'll do whatever I can to make
it my career. I sing because I'm compelled to—not because
I want to be famous or have my picture in the papers. All
I want to do…all I've *ever* wanted to do…is sing. So when
you ask me if my commitment is total, my answer is categorically *yes*!'

By the time she'd finished her impassioned speech Caitlin found herself on the brink of tears. She'd blurted out all
the things she'd never meant to reveal—things about her
past that she really would have preferred to have kept hidden…especially from a man like Jake Sorenson, who probably thought she was an idiot for falling for a loser like
Sean Gates.

But Sean hadn't always been a loser. Once upon a time
he had been the sweetest man in the world, and Caitlin had
believed that she loved him…

'Hey…' Reaching out his hand, Jake gently stroked the
tips of his fingers down her cheek. 'I wasn't casting asper-
sions on your character. I'm sorry if it came out that way.'

The surprisingly feather-light touch made something
clench deep inside her. Recognising it as a hungry need to
be held, she immediately stiffened.

'I'm sorry, too.'

Shaking her head, she automatically moved away in a
bid to resurrect her defences. But as she started walking

again Jake caught up to her, grabbing her arm to make her stop. This time his hold was deliberately firm...*possessive*, almost.

'Don't run away from me. I only want to help you.'

As his intense gaze shot arrows of living blue flame into hers she caught her breath.

'Help me...*how*?'

Bending his head, Jake delivered his answer with a hard, hot kiss that was nothing less than volcanic.

As his lips moved rapaciously over hers, even though she was shocked to her core, Caitlin found herself kissing him back as if her very life depended on it. She even drove her hands through his hair to anchor him to her.

Instinct was like a wild river that had burst its banks and it was near impossible to think about anything above the untamed ferocious beat of her heart...except perhaps to realise that the man kisses were as good as he looked and even *better* than the most erotic fantasy she could imagine...

The delicious sensation of his velvet-textured lips against hers and the warm glide of his tongue in her mouth stirred feelings inside her that she'd never before experienced so wantonly or intensely. *It was during those explosive few moments that Caitlin knew the barriers of safety she'd erected so painstakingly round her heart had come under serious threat...*

Even as she had the realisation Jake brought the kiss to a reluctant end, examining her with a gaze that was more than a little stunned but still very much aroused.

In a low voice he murmured, 'Don't be ashamed because you told me your story. The music business is littered with casualties like your ex-boyfriend. I don't believe that they're bad people. Serious addiction is an illness, not a weakness. Don't shut me out because you've revealed something you wished you hadn't, Caitlin.'

She inhaled sharply and withdrew her hands from his hair. It had started to rain again, and droplets of moisture were settling in quick succession on the silken dark strands that she'd so hungrily slid her fingers into, sparkling there like morning dew.

He sounded so kind and concerned—as if he intimately understood every lash of hurt she had ever suffered and sincerely empathised. Everything about him was almost unbearably seductive, and it made Caitlin ache to lean into him, to perhaps invite another kiss and even ask him to come in for a cup of coffee... But she quickly came to her senses when it hit her just what she was contemplating—and the likely consequences of such a reckless act. *Hadn't she endured enough pain without inviting more?*

She shook her arm free.

'To shut you out I'd first have to let you in, Jake, and I'm not going to do that. Not even if you promised me the earth.'

'Now that it's come to it I don't want to let you go' Lia asserted.

Finishing stirring the mug of coffee she'd made, she brought it over to the small wrought-iron table where the girls sat for lunch. There wasn't a lot of room in the basement, where all the stock was kept, but Lia had had a worktop and sink put in, as well as installing a fridge and a microwave oven, so that the girls could have some hot food from time to time.

Lost in thought, Caitlin was jolted back to the present as the petite blonde pulled out the chair opposite and sat down.

'Sorry, what did you say?'

'I said I don't want to let you go.' Lia breathed out a heavy sigh as she curled her hands round the steaming mug of coffee, her pretty brown eyes not bothering to try and hide her emotion.

Caitlin was genuinely touched. The girls had been friends for a long time now, seeing each other through good times and bad, and it was going to be as much a wrench for Caitlin to relinquish her job as it was for Lia to lose her. She'd always considered the esoteric bookshop to be the best place in the world to work in. Not only was she surrounded by books that had the potential to heal and uplift, but many like-minded people came into the store—and the fact that she worked with her best friend was a blessing.

But for the past week and a half Blue Sky had become more than just a wonderful opportunity to realise a long-held dream. It had become *personal*. Not only had Caitlin grown to respect and admire her fellow musicians, she was also starting to really care about them too. They worked so hard, were passionate about their music, talented and dedicated to their craft, and when Marcie Wallace had walked out they'd been understandably devastated. Caitlin wanted to help put things right...she wanted to help them realise *their* dreams too.

'It's not going to be easy for either of us,' she agreed now, sliding her hand across Lia's. 'But I'm not leaving for good. I might not be working in the shop any more, but that doesn't mean I won't be around. I'll still live here in the village, and when I come home after touring we'll see each other every day because I'll come in and chat and have coffee with you.'

'I know all that.' Lia freed her hand and drove her fingers anxiously through her short blonde hair. 'But if you want to know the truth I've been worrying myself sick about you.'

'Why?' Caitlin was astonished.

'Well...going off with a bunch of strangers to God only knows where. How do you know you can trust these people?'

'Lia, I've got to know them. They're not strangers any more. They're professional musicians. Jake Sorenson, their manager, is—'

'Jake is who I wanted to talk to you about.' The blonde drew a deep breath in. 'Didn't you recognise who he was when you first saw him? Don't you remember there was a "kiss and tell" scandal about him in the papers a few years ago? His wife left him for one of the biggest rock musicians

in the world then spilled the beans about their marriage in
an article in the papers.'

Lia's words started to ring a bell. As memory presented
a helpful picture of the artist her friend had referred to Caitlin stared at the other girl in shock.

'I remember. She left him for Mel Justice…the lead singer
with the band Heart and Soul. I didn't realise the record producer she was married to, was Jake.'

'Well, it was. And the picture she painted of her life
with him wasn't exactly flattering. Did you know she was
a model? Not high-profile, but a familiar face in the magazines just the same. The main reason for the exposé was that
Jake had promised to make her a star and he didn't. Apparently she wanted to give up modelling to become a singer.
But when they got married and he didn't come up with the
goods she had an affair with Mel Justice and eventually divorced Jake to be with him.'

'Then she sold her story to the newspaper,' Caitlin said
quietly.

It jolted her to realise that he'd been married. She hadn't
read the story, but just before Lia had nudged her memory
about what had happened she'd been about to comment that
Jake Sorenson was a true professional—a man who elic-
ited respect and admiration from his peers—and that she
felt very fortunate to have him as a mentor. *But even as the
thought occurred accompanying it was the stirring memory
of last night when Jake had kissed her...*

'Anyway, what has any of what you've just said got to do
with what *I'm* doing, Lia? Why are you digging up old news
about Jake Sorenson?'

'Why? Because I want you to know what you're getting
yourself into that's why'

Lifting her mug of coffee to her lips, her friend agitatedly
put it down again without taking so much as a sip.

'As your best friend, I can't help feeling responsible.
The people in the business you're getting into are open to

all kinds of temptations and bad behaviour. They certainly don't seem to exhibit much loyalty towards each other. I'd hate for you to be associated with the band and have it all backfire on you if the press decide to dig up that kiss and tell story and speculate over if you'll do the same, should anything go wrong.'

'But I'm not having a personal relationship with Jake, am I? I'm only singing with the band he's managing. Plus, I wouldn't dream of selling my story to the press even if I had one! I'm twenty-six, remember? Not some gullible teenager. I can absolutely take care of myself.'

But Caitlin's heart still raced. Nothing Lia had said before had remotely indicated what her friend really felt about her decision to join the band. Up until now she'd been so positive...so encouraging. *'Follow your passion,'* she'd said. *'Don't let anything get in your way.'* Now Caitlin didn't know what to think.

It wasn't any of her business what had or hadn't happened in Jake's marriage. In fact it explained why he sometimes seemed a little aloof. As well as destroying any trust you'd once had for a person, to have your spouse sell their story about your marriage to the papers must have been truly demoralising. But at the end of the day Jake's personal life was nothing remotely to do with her.

'Okay, so if it's true that you can take care of yourself then what about Sean?' Lia's brown eyes sparkled.

Caitlin could hardly believe what she was hearing.

'That was below the belt, Lia,' she murmured. 'Okay, so I've made some wrong turns in my life. Haven't you? Hasn't everyone? It doesn't mean that everything I do is doomed to failure or disaster, does it?'

'I shouldn't have said that. About Sean, I mean.' Lia sniffed. 'I'm sorry, Caitlin. I should know better, considering the business I'm in, shouldn't I? It's just that sometimes it's hard to put wisdom into practice when it comes to someone you care about. You know what men can be like.

They've got a one-track mind when it comes to women like you, and I mean that as a compliment. You're beautiful and talented, with a sweet and trusting nature. They're bound to try and take advantage and here you are—going off into the wide blue yonder with five of them!'

'Well, you've got to try and stop worrying, Lia. I'm going to be just fine. I'm doing what I want to do, right? Nobody is forcing me. If I can trust that everything will be okay, then why can't you?'

Abruptly rising to her feet, Caitlin carried her empty mug over to the sink. Then she rinsed it out and turned it upside down on the drainer.

'I'd better get back upstairs and relieve Nicky so that she can have her lunch. Today's my last day at the shop, so let's not spoil it by having an argument.'

'I'm sorry. I'm just feeling a bit on edge because you're going. Don't be mad at me?' Lia pleaded as she got to her feet.

'Don't be silly!' Grinning, Caitlin fondly ruffled her hair. 'How on earth could I be mad at you for caring? Since that particular commodity has been sadly lacking in my life for quite some time, I can assure you I'm open to all the TLC I can get!'

But even as she laughed off her friend's concern Caitlin couldn't help dwelling on what she'd said about Jake. The revelation about Jake's former marriage perturbed her. She didn't often read the celebrity gossip that littered the newspapers and social media, and right now she was glad that she didn't. Whatever had happened between Jake and his ex-wife, it must have been painful for both of them, she reasoned. She should just focus on singing with the band and not concern herself with how Blue Sky's manager might or might not conduct himself in private.

CHAPTER FOUR

AT THE END of an emotionally fraught day, Caitlin sank back into a hot steamy bath and exhaled a heartfelt sigh. Flickering candles cast dancing shadows on the walls of the small, once shabby bathroom she'd sought to transform with some pink paint, pale blue curtains and accessories. She was genuinely pleased with what she'd achieved.

Closing her eyes, she breathed in the exotic perfume that filled the air from the scented candles and her favourite aromatic bath oil. Trailing her fingers idly in the water, she let her thoughts whirl. Electing to leave her job, she hadn't exactly burnt her bridges, reflected, because Lia had promised she could have a job with her any day. But it was still a scary thought to realise that she was giving up something relatively stable and secure for something that was its direct antithesis.

Splashing a handful of water across her shoulders, Caitlin opened her eyes and absently watched the droplets roll down her warm, scented skin. Frowning, she thought about the afternoon's rehearsals and how Jake had regularly berated her for lack of concentration—not to mention for pretty much everything else. He'd yelled at her so often that the rest of the crew had cast each other quizzical glances, as if to ask, *what's going on?*

Was he behaving like that because he regretted kissing her? She hadn't *asked* him to kiss her! Her concentration might well not have been what it should, but despite the rights or wrongs of that inflammatory kiss how did the man *expect* her to react when she'd just left the job that she'd been devoted to for the past five years? It just wasn't that easy to detach herself from a person or a place she cared about.

At least Rick and the others had been more understanding. They had even brought along a bottle of champagne to celebrate her 'release', although Jake had declined to join them in their impromptu toast during the break. Instead, he'd collected his leather jacket and gone out for a while… 'To get some fresh air,' he'd tersely explained.

'Blast you, Jake Sorenson! I'm doing my best here. Give me a break, can't you?'

Grabbing the innocent plastic yellow duck bobbing about on the water, she flung it down in temper. It made a very sad little splash. Not nearly enough impact to vent the anger that was bubbling up inside her.

Then, as if on cue, the doorbell rang.

Caitlin cursed out loud, determined to ignore it. But when it rang for a second and then a third time her resolve crumbled and she hauled herself out of the bath, grabbed the blue terry robe off the peg behind the door and struggled into it, littering the air with vague mutterings of irritation as she did so…

Stomping through the living room, then down the cold linoleum-covered stairs, she wondered who could be so inconsiderate and foolhardy enough to disrupt one of her favourite pastimes.

'Jake.'

All the strength seemed to drain from her limbs as she came face to face with her unexpected visitor. His lean, athletic frame was clothed entirely in black, and his long legs and broad shoulders were outlined by the filtered orange glow of a nearby street lamp. No other man had the power to disturb her as much. Jake had a presence that scrambled her thoughts into a muddled tangle and almost made it hard to breathe. All compelling lean angles and shadows, his gorgeous cheekbones were almost impossibly perfect.

Meeting his bold gaze, she asked, 'What is it? Is something wrong?'

'Can I come in?'

Because the request had caught her off guard, Caitlin found herself nodding. Then she stepped back into the dimly lit hallway, with its unfortunate flocked gold wallpaper and worn red carpet, to let him enter. The damp hair that she'd screwed up so carelessly into an improvised knot hung loose and heavy behind her head and several long ebony strands had worked free to glance against her cheek. Beneath her robe her body was still slick with moisture because she hadn't had time to dry herself. And she was stark naked beneath that robe...

It was a fact that did little to add to her confidence. Not when Jake edged past her with an enigmatic little smile that made all the strength ooze out of her limbs like sherbet through a straw.

'Up the stairs,' she instructed weakly as he turned and waited while she closed the front door.

Glancing briefly up the narrow staircase that led to her flat, he said, 'You go first.'

Caitlin had been afraid he might say that. With her face burning she squeezed past him, inadvertently inhaling the heady scents of cedarwood and leather and the fresh smell of the outdoors that clung to him as her body brushed briefly against his. It was like coming into contact with a power supply, she thought as she began to ascend the stairs. There wasn't a cell in her body that hadn't felt the effect.

Every step she took in her slim bare feet with their scarlet-painted toenails was pure *agony* because she was acutely aware of Jake, just inches behind her. The belt round her waist had been fastened so tightly he couldn't fail to be apprised of her shape beneath the perfectly innocent terry robe, and Caitlin squirmed inwardly all the way up into her living room.

'Come in,' she invited.

His heart thudding, because his senses were still infused with the memory of their kiss the other night, Jake trained his gaze on his surroundings in a bid to divert his aroused recollection.

He immediately registered what had once been an ornate Victorian fireplace that was now home to a small electric heater that surely wasn't big enough to heat the whole room. There was a large pink ceramic vase with palm fronds in it just to the side of the hearth, and a large squashy red sofa with multi-coloured cushions arranged against the wall. Above it was a large gold-framed print of *Flaming June* by Frederic Leighton. The vivid orange of the lady's dress was clinging like a sunburst to her pale reposing figure.

Jake absorbed all of this in just a few short seconds, but inevitably his gaze was helplessly drawn back to Caitlin. In her charming state of *dishabille*, how could it not be? What *was* that scent she was wearing?

With her face scrubbed clean of make-up, her silky black hair escaping all attempts at confinement, and wearing nothing but a plain terry robe, to Jake she was temptation personified. If she had the power to make him hot when she was dressed in tight jeans and a T-shirt it was nothing compared to the effect she was having on him in her present get-up. He just prayed that her pretty green eyes wouldn't stray far south of his stomach, because right then he was fighting a losing battle to keep his lustful stirrings to himself.

So much for his promise to maintain a professional distance. He'd already broken that vow by stealing that incendiary kiss the other night. One taste of pure, unadulterated heaven had ensured that sooner or later he would be back for more. He'd already had to make himself scarce once this afternoon, because two hours of Caitlin up on the stage wiggling her hips as she sang, her breasts bouncing ever so slightly in her hot pink T-shirt, had almost made him crazy with want. Professing a need for some fresh air had just been a handy euphemism for what he really needed…a cold shower so icy it would freeze an ordinary mortal into a cryogenic trance.

When Jake didn't immediately speak, Caitlin nervously wiped her hands down her robe and motioned vaguely towards the sofa. 'Why don't you sit down? I just need to go and dress. I was having a bath when you rang the bell.'

'Don't get dressed on my account,' her visitor drawled, making no discernible move to sit down.

Her face flamed red.

'I'm still wet,' she gulped, immediately wishing she could take back her innocently meant remark, because Jake's glance was all but stripping her naked. Want, need and lust swirled between them. 'I mean I need…'

Caitlin's hand trembled as she saw Jake's eyes grow tellingly dark. Now his glance was focused on her mouth, on the soft, plump lower lip that her tongue had just innocently dampened.

'What are we going to do, Caitlin?' he asked softly, his gravelly voice reeling her in with its disturbing undisguised intonation of heat and sex.

'Do about what?'

'About *us*. Don't pretend you don't know what I mean. For God's sake, the kiss we shared the other night when I walked you home was no innocent kiss goodnight. I got the distinct impression that you enjoyed it as much as I did. Was I wrong?'

'Look, I really need to go and put some clothes on. If you wait here I'll make us some coffee once I'm dressed and then we can talk.'

Jake smiled. She was gazing at him as though hypnotised. As she studied him her bewitching emerald eyes were dazzled—*glazed*, almost. Whatever she felt about him, she couldn't deny there was a combustible attraction between them. And he couldn't think of another woman who had the ability to send his pulse sky-rocketing and his libido raging with just a simple glance.

It wasn't just her beauty that drew him to her. There was a refreshing innocence about Caitlin. Having met so many women whose hunger for fame and success made them employ any means possible to get what they wanted—*his ex-wife being a case in point*—he found Caitlin was like a breath of fresh air. Jake had never wanted a woman more in his life...wanted her with an ache that was the sweetest agony from the moment he woke up in the morning to when he lay down to sleep at night.

'Good. Because it won't go away,' he continued. 'Sooner or later we're going to have to deal with it.'

Caitlin's already pink cheeks flushed even pinker. Then she turned and fled into the bedroom to get dressed.

Sighing, Jake dropped down onto the squashy red sofa, picked up a cushion, then angrily jettisoned it onto the floor. *Just what the hell did he think he was doing?* He'd called in on her because he'd wanted to apologise for being so uncompromising at rehearsals, but as soon as he'd set eyes on her in that innocent terry robe of hers he'd known immediately that she wasn't wearing anything underneath it. Somehow his rigidly imposed self-control had gone out of the window and all he'd been able to think about was how soon he could get her into bed.

He wanted to bury himself so deep inside her he'd assuage every ache he'd ever had...*hers* too. Yes, he'd had the odd one-night stand since Jodie had done the dirty on him—how else could he satisfy a healthy libido—but nothing could have prepared him for a hunger so primal, so insatiable, that it threatened to consume him body and soul if it wasn't satisfied.

Dragging his fingers through his hair, Jake slowly shook his head. To add to his frustration Caitlin's provocative scent lingered in the room, tormenting him. Where was she, for goodness' sake? How long did it take to throw some clothes on? *Longer than it would take him to tear them off that was for sure...*

Restless, he got to his feet, his long legs taking him to the other side of the room and back again as he paced the floor. The living room was ridiculously small—almost oppressively so. A few family photos sat on the mantelpiece, along with a small glass jar full of assorted coloured crystals.

Jake was far too distracted to examine the photographs more closely, so he turned away to survey the rest of the room. A large pine bookcase dominated an entire wall, and there wasn't a shelf on it that wasn't crammed to bursting point with books. He barely stole a glance at the titles he was so keyed up, but he couldn't fail to notice that most of the literature dwelt on self-development or philosophy.

Had Caitlin been interested in those subjects before or *after* her catastrophic relationship with the drug addict? Jake was curious. Clearly she must have been driven to seek out some sort of guidance after such an ordeal. Somehow he felt chastened. Living with a drug addict and alcoholic would certainly be no picnic. He himself had had friends and associates who'd been drawn down a similar destructive route. He'd told Caitlin that the music business was full of such casualties.

But she'd confessed to him that she'd lost everything, including her home. That must surely be the reason why she was living in this *rabbit hutch*. Jake would go stir crazy, living in such a confined space. Being the grateful owner of spacious homes in London, New York and LA—which were admittedly empty most of the time, due to his peripatetic lifestyle—he doubted he would manage even half as well if he had to live the way Caitlin did. Even his room at the quaint Pilgrim's Inn was three times the size of this one.

Without realising it, his hands had curled into fists down by his sides.

He'd remarked to her that addiction was a disease, not

a weakness, but by God he'd like just ten minutes with the jerk who'd ripped her off so badly that she was reduced to living in two shabby rented rooms.

'What would you like to drink? Tea or coffee?'

Caitlin's voice took Jake by surprise. Turning round, he avidly noted her long shapely legs, which were encased in soft worn denim, and the pretty pink top she'd donned, which was fastened at the front with little pearl buttons. In her apparent haste to get dressed the top two buttons had been left undone, inadvertently revealing the creamy cleft between her breasts, and the arresting sight made him catch his breath.

But she might not have left the buttons undone deliberately—she hardly needed to resort to feminine wiles to get his attention. All the woman had to do was glance at him with those bewitching emerald eyes and Jake was all hers.

'Neither,' he answered. 'Why don't you just come and sit down so we can talk?'

Caitlin acquiesced, her brows puckering when she noticed that one of her multi-coloured cushions was lying on the floor. Inside her chest, her heart was galloping at what felt like a worrying breakneck speed.

When Jake had asserted that sooner or later they would have to 'deal with it', had he been saying that it was inevitable that they had an affair? Because if he had then he hadn't reckoned with her iron will. It didn't matter how attracted she was to the man, she wasn't the type to jump thoughtlessly into bed with him. Sean was the only man she'd ever been intimate with, and to be honest it hadn't been anything to write home about even when she'd foolishly imagined herself in love with him.

Being a singer and a member of Blue Sky was far more important than having a hot little affair with the band's manager, she told herself.

'I was rough on you today.' Still standing in the centre

of the room, Jake rubbed a hand round his beard-darkened jaw. 'I feel like I owe you an apology.'

'Why?'

'Because I pushed you too hard.' He flinched as though genuinely regretting it.

'You don't have to apologise. I know I've still got a long way to go and I need all the help and guidance I can get. Rick says that you're the best, and so do the others. I'm hungry to learn, Jake. You shouldn't lose any sleep over the fact that you had to yell at me a few times.'

Gritting his teeth, he silently cursed the ache in his groin that refused to be tamped. *It wasn't the fact that he'd lost his temper a few times that he was losing sleep over.* She was sitting on her sofa, looking about as tempting as Eve in the Garden of Eden, and her soothing velvet voice rolled over him like honey. She might not know it but she was seducing him as thoroughly as if she sat there naked, beckoning him to come to her.

'Are you always this reasonable?' He quirked an eyebrow.

Although he'd apologised, he was still spoiling for an argument—*anything* to defuse the sexually charged tension between them.

'No.' An amused smile played at the corners of her mouth. 'Sean used to accuse me of being unreasonable all the time.'

'Sean?'

'My ex-boyfriend.'

'The drug addict.' Jake hadn't meant to sound cruel, but the fact was he wasn't in the mood to be magnanimous. A stab of jealousy had sliced through his insides at Caitlin's reference to the man she'd previously been in a relationship with.

Suddenly rising to her feet, she let her fingers toy restlessly with the little pearl buttons on her blouse. The gesture inevitably drew his gaze.

'Amongst other things he was a painter and decorator by trade. Not that he was in work very often…For obvious reasons.' Her expression was briefly pained. 'But, like you said, just because he was an addict, it didn't mean he was a bad person. He was easily led by some unsavoury friends, that was the trouble.'

Caitlin dipped her head and Jake found himself automatically taking a step towards her.

'So, you were "unreasonable" because you tried to warn him off those so-called friends?'

'Yes... That and because I didn't give him money as often as he liked to buy his drugs. I was struggling to keep the roof over our heads as it was. I had a lovely flat that I'd bought with a legacy my grandmother had left me and I was eventually forced to sell it because of Sean. He was in so much debt due to his drug habit.'

'And where is he now?' he asked. *A million miles away, he hoped.* Outer Mongolia wouldn't be far enough.

'When we broke up he said he was going to London. His brother lives there and he was going to stay with him to try and straighten himself out. I hope for his sake he was able to. But, that said, I'm just so glad he's out of my life. Being with him had me fearing for my sanity. I hardly knew who I was any more. Sometimes I can't believe what a fool I was to trust him and believe that he would change. One thing's for sure...I'll never give my trust so easily to a man again.'

Her emerald eyes glistened briefly and Jake swallowed hard. He hated the idea that she wasted even a *second* of her time thinking about her ex and what he had put her through.

'Anyway, I don't know why I'm standing here telling you all this,' she finished.

'I asked you to. What about your family? Were they supportive when they found out what was going on?'

'My parents and my brother are in America. He moved out there first and they followed. They've started up a business out there. Anyway...'

With a shrug Caitlin briefly met his eyes and then looked quickly away again.

'I didn't want them to worry about me so I didn't tell them. I made my bed and I had to lie in it. They gave me the chance of going with them when they left but I opted not to take it. Besides, they always taught me it was important to stand on my own two feet, and I wasn't going to go running to them the moment I was in trouble. I wanted to prove to myself and to them that I could turn my life around and be proud of myself.'

'Whilst that's commendable, I thought families were supposed to help each other out when one of them was in trouble?'

'Do yours? Help you when you're in trouble I mean?'

Jake hadn't expected her to turn the question on him. For a dizzying moment he found himself awash in a sea of feelings that he usually tried to submerge...feelings of pain, confusion and a sickening sense of being abandoned by life.

His mouth drying, he answered, 'No... They don't. They *can't*. I don't know who they are. I was raised in a children's home.'

Caitlin's bewitching green eyes immediately softened. 'Oh, Jake...I'm so sorry.'

The suggestion of concerned sympathy in her voice was like a gun pointed straight at his heart. He immediately sought to deflect it.

'Don't be. I learned very quickly not to depend on anyone else for either my happiness or my wellbeing. I survived the experience—that's all you need to know. That's all *anyone* needs to know.'

Twisting her hands together, she took a few moments before commenting, 'You've done more than just survive, Jake. You've made an amazing success of your life.'

'Is that how it looks to you?' The question was painfully ironic.

'Anyway, regarding my own family, we're...let's just say we respect our differences. They have their life and I have mine.'

'You mean you haven't told them that you've joined the band?'

'I will tell them…eventually. But, just not right now.'

Jake shrugged. 'It's your call.'

'You said that you learned not to depend on anyone else to make you happy. What about romantic relationships, Jake? Have you had maybe one or two that haven't worked out?'

'Who *hasn't?*'

A reticent smile suggested that discussing his own experiences was the last thing he wanted to do. It wasn't hard to understand why he should feel that way. Nobody welcomed talking about the things that had hurt them. Yet Caitlin couldn't help wanting to know more. *Despite her vow never to easily trust another man, the idea of perhaps trusting Jake was strangely compelling.* After all, he knew what it was like to have been badly hurt by someone and wouldn't knowingly inflict similar hurt on someone else…would he?

Drawing in a deep breath for courage, she asked the question she'd been longing to hear the answer to since talking to Lia.

'My friend Lia—the manager of the shop where I worked—she told me that she once read in the papers that you'd been married.'

As Caitlin had expected, Jake's guard slammed down like a portcullis. 'Then why ask if I've had any relationships that haven't worked out? It must be obvious that my marriage didn't, if your friend read about it.'

He let loose an irritated sigh, but Caitlin detected weariness in the sound, as if he was well and truly sick of the subject.

'Presumably she also told you that my wife left me and then sold a sordid little tale to the press?'

She flushed, feeling uncomfortably guilty. 'Yes…she did.'

'Then that should tell you it was hardly a match made in heaven. My ex was a manipulative little liar…what else do you want to know?'

'Please don't be so defensive. I was hoping you might tell me your side of the story. I never read any details myself. To be honest, I didn't even recognise you when we first met. I don't often read the newspapers, and neither do I use social media very much. I honestly won't breathe a word of this conversation to anyone...not even to my friend.'

'I take it I have your word on that?' Jake's blue eyes were momentarily fierce.

With her heart thudding, Caitlin nodded. 'Of course.'

'Her name was Jodie and she was a model who wanted to become a pop singer. I had no idea of her ambition at the time. Anyway, we met at a party and had a few dates. She was pretty and engaging enough to capture my attention, and on a weekend break to Rome I foolishly asked her to marry me.'

He shook his head in mocking disbelief.

'Practically as soon as we were married she started to put pressure on me to help her get a record deal...all the while telling me I was the best thing that had ever happened to her and that she was madly in love with me, of course. You'd think I would have known better.'

He gave a harsh self-deprecating laugh before continuing.

'She couldn't sing, and when she realised I wasn't going to help further her career she started an affair with Mel Justice—the lead guitarist of the bestselling rock band on the planet. I was travelling in South America on business when she moved in with him and on my return she told me she was filing for divorce. Then, when the case came to court, she cited mental cruelty because I'd allegedly promised to help make her a star and I hadn't...'

The way Jake shook his head told Caitlin everything she needed to know about how he'd felt about that.

'In the story she portrayed me as some kind of Svengali who'd preyed on her naïvety and led her astray. If it hadn't been so painful and hadn't ruined my reputation it would have been funny. Anyway, with the help of a high-profile

American lawyer, courtesy of her new boyfriend, she got her divorce and was awarded a ridiculous sum of money from me for so-called damages. Then she married her lover and became Mrs Justice.'

Jake's telling of the painful events was succinct and to the point. But to have had his reputation sullied by Jodie's lies and for her to have sold her story to the newspapers because she hadn't got what she wanted out of him must have seriously shattered his belief in relationships. Sighing, Caitlin tucked some drifting strands of hair behind her ear.

Relieved to have done with his story, Jake moved across to the sofa to join her. Breathing out on a sigh, he gently touched his knuckles to the side of her cheek. *As soon as he'd done it he knew he was lost.*

Even though he'd kissed her, touching Caitlin was still a revelation. Her skin had the texture of the purest silk. An erotic image of her lying naked in his bed, her slender limbs tangled in black satin sheets, her eyes dark with desire and her skin flushed pink with arousal, slipped easily into his mind to taunt him even more. He wanted to touch her everywhere. He wouldn't rush. He'd take his time and savour every inch of her beautiful body, every flavour. Was she uninhibitedly vocal? Or would she whimper gently when he brought her to climax?

'Anyway, I think I've said enough. Thanks for telling me about Sean. I hope it hasn't upset you too much?' It didn't surprise him when his voice sounded less than steady.

'It hasn't. I'm fine.' Caitlin willed herself to move, to put herself out of reach of his seductive touch and wrest her gaze from the haunting blue eyes that made her feel so restless and hungry.

She burned for him. Could Jake see that? Could he tell? If she was going to make her dream come true she couldn't afford to let him know just how much she desired him. Becoming intimately involved with Jake Sorenson would be a disaster personally *and* professionally. Somehow she had to play it cool…for *both* their sakes. They were both recovering from seriously hurtful relationships and, if nothing else, they should exercise some common sense.

'I'm just very tired.' Faking a yawn, Caitlin surprised herself by following it up with a genuine one.

Jake immediately got to his feet. Planting his hands either side of his straight lean hips, he nodded. 'I almost forgot how late it was.'

He should be glad of the excuse to leave. *He didn't dare risk staying for much longer because being with Caitlin was putting an impossible strain on him to stick to his vow to leave well alone.*

'I know we haven't discussed the situation we've got but that will have to wait. At the end of the day, the band is the first priority. I'll see you tomorrow at rehearsals. Three o'clock, usual place.'

'I'll be there.' Caitlin pushed to her feet.

'Good. I'll see myself out. Don't come down.'

Following him onto the landing, Caitlin felt every muscle in her body tense as she stared at his back, at the soft leather jacket that accommodated his broad shoulders to perfection, at his long, hard-muscled legs and taut, lean behind. A wave of heat rolled over her and almost made her lose her balance. She'd never ogled a man in her life before, but there was something about Jake Sorenson that made her behave out of character…something wild and untamed.

She'd stared down into a yawning abyss of darkness many times during those two hellish years with Sean, and had lost count of the times she'd prayed for her life to be 'normal'. But, in truth, she'd always known that she could never be content with a conventional nine-to-five existence. She needed more than that…*much* more. That was why she'd shown up for the audition with Blue Sky. That was why she was willing to kiss goodbye to the sleepy little village that had been her home and that was why she wanted to take her chances with Jake and the others…

'Jake?'

Coming to a standstill at the bottom of the stairs, he glanced up at her. As she stared back into his fathomless blue eyes Caitlin mused that it was like falling into the sky.

'Thanks for dropping by and for…for our little chat.'

'No problem.'

Conveying that he was in a hurry, Jake abruptly opened the door and slammed it shut behind him.

CHAPTER FIVE

THE BLAST OF a car horn sounding right outside her front door made Caitlin jump. In the throes of getting ready for her evening out, she glanced at the clock on the mantel and saw that it was later than she'd thought.

Softly cursing, she yanked her hairbrush roughly through her sable hair, then quickly painted her lips with the new plum shade of lipstick she'd bought. Her hand was a little unsteady as she applied it and, to make matters even worse, she decided that the colour was a little too dramatic for her liking. But she was just going to have to grin and bear it. She was already feeling tense at the distinct possibility of being chastised yet again for lateness. That would make it the third time this week and it might just be the straw that broke the camel's back as far as Jake was concerned.

Hurriedly snatching her leather jacket off the couch and pulling it on, she grabbed her purse, shoved it into a pocket and flew down the steep, narrow staircase as if the hounds of hell themselves were after her. Her breath hitched as she hurried towards the ominous-looking black Jeep, its engine running.

Jake leaned across and pushed open the passenger door. 'Hi,' he greeted her.

His expression didn't give much away, and it couldn't help but increase the overall sense of trepidation that Caitlin was feeling. They were going to see a band tonight and would be spending a large amount of time together...*alone*.

She didn't doubt the experience was going to be a real test for them both.

'Hi.' There were three seats in the front of the vehicle and she automatically sat next to the window and slammed the door shut.

'I want you next to me.'

'What?'

The slow burning heat from Jake's gaze almost scorched Caitlin where she sat. He didn't embellish the comment. He didn't *have* to. They both knew only too well why he wanted her to sit closer to him. *Could day resist following night?* She'd have loved to have had a handy reason with which to refuse him, but her mind was worryingly bereft of anything helpful as his arresting blue eyes entrapped hers.

With thumping heart she murmured, 'Feeling lonely, are we?' Then, before he could reply, she somehow found herself sitting in the luxuriously upholstered leather seat next to his.

His lips lifted in a grin.

'Not any more.'

'Well, I'm glad that I've made you happy.' Her dark hair brushed against her reddened cheekbone as she bent to buckle her seatbelt. 'For *once*.'

Chuckling, Jake put the car into gear and steered it smoothly away from the kerb. It should have reassured her that he seemed to be in a particularly good mood tonight, but it didn't make things any easier. *Not when she was already gripped by the familiar disturbing waves of disorientation and desire that seemed to be inevitable whenever they were together.* And all day that combustible kiss they'd shared when he'd walked her home from the pub had played over and over in her mind.

Their attraction for each other had been growing stronger and stronger. It only needed the tiniest spark to turn it into a conflagration. It was made even more acute now, by the intimate space they shared in the car.

Caitlin couldn't help stealing a covetous glance at Jake

as he drove. True to form, he was clothed in his habitual black, with no apparent concessions to dressing up for their night out—although he didn't need to wear fancy clothes to draw a woman's eye. *Not when he exuded charisma simply by breathing.* Add to that, he had the intriguing persona of a man who'd been around musicians for most of his life and had seen it all…group bust-ups, wrecked hotel rooms, drink, drugs, groupies and corrupt management…and had lived to tell the tale. Jake had been there, done that, and worn the T-shirt.

Sighing, Caitlin smoothed her hand down over her jeans and couldn't help wondering what people would see in her when she finally took to the stage to sing. Would they quickly categorise her as just another starstruck wannabe? A wide-eyed innocent without much experience of anything at all? *If they did, then they couldn't be more wrong.* How could they know the narrow escape she'd had from the kind of destructive relationship that most mothers of daughters had nightmares about? Consequently, she was far from ignorant about the pitfalls that awaited girls who were too trusting, who kidded themselves that they could 'fix' a partner's problems simply by loving them enough. *Caitlin had found to her cost that that was one of the biggest lies believed by women.*

Jake must have sensed her shudder and he turned his head in surprise. 'Are you okay?'

'Yes, I'm fine.'

Obviously deciding not to pander to any sense of insecurity she might be feeling, he drawled, 'I trust your clothes aren't going to turn into rags if I don't get you home by midnight?'

He was, of course, referring to her habit of turning in early if she could. Caitlin's cheeks seared pink with embarrassment. Early nights free from anxiety had been denied her in the days when she'd waited up for Sean, praying he hadn't got himself into more trouble. If she'd had a pound for every prayer she'd uttered in those two harsh, unhappy years she'd be a rich woman.

When he hadn't come home when expected Caitlin had hoped the police hadn't got him in a cell somewhere, or that some drug dealer he owed money to hadn't beaten him up, or worse. When he'd lied to her yet again, let her down or stolen money from her, she'd prayed hard for the strength to cope—still foolishly believing that she could somehow rescue him from the dark road he'd been intent on travelling down. But when he'd started to bully her, threaten her and finally *hit* her, she'd dug deep for the strength to end the relationship before it ended *her*.

The bottom line was she wasn't about to apologise to Jake for something that had been an important part of her emotional recovery, no matter how much he scorned her early nights.

'There's about as much likelihood of that as you turning into Prince Charming any time soon,' she muttered.

To her astonishment, she actually detected a smile on Jake's lips. It was only slight, and a less sensitive person might have missed it, but she was so intimately attuned to the man's every unconscious gesture and nuance she couldn't help but be aware of it. It did funny things to her insides that 'almost' smile of his, not to mention other sensitive areas of her body...

Pursing her lips, she stared determinedly ahead of her as a sudden fierce shower of rain sheeted the windscreen's glass, temporarily obliterating the view until Jake switched on the wipers.

'And there was I, hoping we'd get a clear night with a romantic moon and starlight,' he quipped.

'Is that really what you were hoping for?'

Lifting a shoulder, he smiled again, this time more freely. 'Why? You don't think I have it in me to be romantic?'

The remark immediately threw her.

'How would I know? I don't know you well enough.'

'Then it's clearly time for me to do something about that, don't you think?'

He didn't turn his head to look at her. The provocative words were simply left hanging in the air between them, like a small but lethal incendiary device.

Urgently feeling the need to change the conversation to something far less dangerous, Caitlin asked, 'So, who's the band we're going to see tonight? You didn't tell me.'

'They're called Ace of Hearts. The lead singer is Nikki Drake and I'd really like you to see her. She isn't what you might call the best singer in the world, but what she lacks in vocal range she more than makes up for in her performance. It's electrifying. She lives and breathes the band and it shows.'

'And you're hoping that I might pick up a few tips?'

The rain ceased as suddenly as it had started, and as the wipers squeaked redundantly across the screen Jake's brief azure glance at Caitlin was like a heat-seeking missile that went straight to her womb.

'Sure,' he answered.

Jake was amazed that he'd even got the word out. Whenever he caught sight of Caitlin's bewitching face—whether by design or by accident—he was all but struck dumb. Ever since he'd kissed her he'd been filled with an insatiable desire to know her intimately. As far as he was concerned, not having to share her company with anyone else tonight was like being given the keys to heaven.

For a man that prided himself on always being in control of situations, his feelings for this woman were unravelling him. If he didn't act soon to counteract the danger then the walls he'd built around his heart, brick by brick, would come crashing down and render him helpless. Whilst he would do everything in his power not to let that happen, there was no reason why he shouldn't take Caitlin to bed to help get her out of his system...*was there?*

'Do you know her well? Nikki Drake, I mean?' she probed.

Hearing the curiosity in her voice, Jake smiled. He smiled because he detected the unspoken question that she *really* wanted to ask, which was *How well do you know her?* Although he'd never been remotely attracted to Nikki, he couldn't help but experience a certain male satisfaction at the idea that Caitlin might be a little jealous.

'I know her well enough. But then, I know a lot of people in my business,' he drawled.

Not for the first time Caitlin realised that Jake was a man of few words. But, whatever he said, there was always a wealth of meaning behind it that often required some serious detective work. Then again, perhaps she should just go with the flow and not worry too much about what he meant. Jake was Jake: enigmatic, taciturn, not giving an inch. She'd better get used to it if she was going to make a half decent job of working with him.

But what she wouldn't give for him to one day speak about *her* in the same admiring way that he spoke about Nikki Drake... She was feeling ridiculously jealous of the woman when she hadn't even seen her or heard her sing yet.

'Then I can't wait to see her,' she remarked, hoping that the amiable smile she gave would convince him that she meant it.

There wasn't a single gaze in the room that wasn't trained on the sexy strutting singer onstage. A small shapely blonde, her blue eyes heavily outlined with thick black liner, her generous mouth painted with bold red lipstick, Nikki Drake held the mike as if she owned it and commanded the small raised stage with every sexy thrust of her hips, every husky note that she sang.

Her slender body was encased in tight black satin and a wide scarlet belt was cinched tightly round her impossibly tiny waist. Her creamy breasts were clearly enhanced by the loving support of a daring uplift bra *Sex on legs,* as her friend Lia might say.

The performance was riveting. While the music throbbed around them Caitlin experienced an adrenaline rush like nothing she'd ever experienced before at a live concert. Was this how Jake wanted her to look? Commanding, sexy, wearing tight, hard-to-breathe-in clothing specifically designed to highlight every curve, every undulation? Unashamedly putting everything she had on show?

Her throat was dry from the combined heat of wall-to-wall people crammed into a space not much bigger than a living room. Taking a hasty sip of her rum and Coke, with the ice in the glass already melted to slivers, Caitlin almost jumped out of her skin when Jake moved up behind her. Her senses reeled with shock when his lean, hard body was all of a sudden on intimate terms with her back, his denim-clad thighs carelessly brushing the backs of hers as his warm, bourbon-laced breath drifted tantalisingly over her hair. Caitlin went rigid.

'What do you think?' he asked, and the husky timbre of his voice did seriously X-rated things to her body, draining her limbs of all their strength in the process.

'About—about what?' She could barely squeeze the words past her throat.

'About Nikki and the band of course. What did you think I meant?'

Jake's amused smile was almost tangible. She didn't need to see it to know that he was taking great pleasure in teasing her. She was suddenly grateful for the dim lighting and the intimate proximity of the other bodies around her, because she didn't want him to see that her face was burning.

'She's very good. They're all very talented. I'm really enjoying the music,' she told him.

'Without a doubt you're a better singer,' Jake responded. 'All we have to do now is find the right image for you.'

'As long as you don't expect me to pour myself into tight black satin. I'll definitely draw the line at *that*.'

To bolster her flagging courage, Caitlin tipped up her glass and drained the entire contents of the drink that remained. Her head swam a little as the alcohol hit home, but it was as nothing compared to the dizziness she was already experiencing with Jake getting closer by the second.

'I think we should go for something more classy. *Sexy…* but classy.'

His hand drifted over her hip to settle on her waist, his fingers deliberately sliding across the thin silk of the white camisole she wore beneath her jacket. Caitlin almost stopped breathing.

When she lifted her hand, ostensibly to move his away, his fingers caught hers and trapped them possessively. The words she'd started to form were suddenly obliterated as she closed her mouth, shut her eyes and sensed Jake press even closer. A tremulous shudder went through her as he brushed her hair aside and planted a devastatingly erotic kiss on the sensitive juncture between her shoulder and neck.

The unexpected caress went straight to her core and almost made her whimper with pleasure. *It was as though he had branded her.* Beneath the flimsy fabric of her strapless bra her nipples turned rigid and achy and her legs turned seriously weak. Thank God for the music and the crowd, because if they'd been alone right then Caitlin was certain her defences against such a passionate assault on her senses would have been zero.

Desperately needing to regain her composure, she straightened and turned round to face Jake. But the message his compelling blue eyes were conveying drove every coherent thought in her head straight out again.

'Don't. Please don't.'

Even as she softly uttered the words she thought they didn't make sense. *She* made no sense. Half plea, half whisper, they were carried away by the hypnotic beat of the music, by the laughter of the couple standing next to them, a young man with his arms firmly round his pretty Titian-haired girlfriend as they swayed together to the music.

'Please don't what?' Jake caught her hand and unhesitatingly drew her in tight to his chest.

Such eyes he had, Caitlin thought feverishly…piercing blue-grey, like mist swirling over a storm-ravaged sea…

Holding Caitlin against him was the most exquisite pleasure bordering on pain that Jake had ever experienced. Her soft yet slender curves fitted his embrace as though she'd been made for just that purpose.

The sound of the throbbing music, the approving cheers of the audience, the chink of glasses from the bar and the soporific scent of incense that hung over them like a heady cloud—they all faded away, leaving Jake with nothing but his overwhelming need for the woman in front of him.

His desire to make Caitlin his own in the most primal way a man and a woman could consummate their lust was testing him to the very limit. Already he was hurtling close to the edge of that self-imposed control. He knew he shouldn't want her so much. Professionally, it had disaster written all over it, and personally he wasn't ready to trust a woman. After what Jodie had done trust didn't come easily. Both those reasons should make him stay well clear.

With a supreme test of will, Jake slid his hands up to Caitlin's shoulders, where he briefly let them linger. Then he gently but firmly moved her away. Her eyes instantly registered surprise and confusion and Jake cursed himself for torturing them both.

'I don't want to hurt you,' he murmured.

Caitlin bit her lip and inclined her head in a brief nod. Then she turned back to watch the band, crossing her arms over her chest as if to protect herself. Her beautiful hair cascaded down her back like the most luxurious black silk and Jake ached with every fibre of his being to reach out and touch it. He had been captivated by women before, but not like this—*never* like this.

What he needed right now was another drink. He'd have to be careful not to exceed the limit, because he was driving, and even another drink would be no consolation for his present sexual frustration. Sensibly, he decided against it. Instead, he stayed put to watch the band and decide which elements of the performance he could point out to Caitlin that might help her when the time came for her to make her debut with Blue Sky.

'Hey, that was good. Where did you learn to play guitar like that?'

Mike Casey sat cross-legged on the living room floor, barefooted and tousled-haired, his guitar resting easily against his thighs. His brown eyes regarded Caitlin in admiration. She'd just given him a personal rendition of a well-known singer's most iconic track, with all its attendant complicated chord changes and a few innovative ones of her own. He wondered if Jake or Rick had heard her play yet, because Caitlin didn't just play a 'little', as she'd modestly confessed at her audition. The woman knew her way round a guitar as if the instrument were a natural extension of her own graceful hands.

Setting down her guitar to take a sip from the soft drink Mike had given her, she answered, 'I had lessons when I was younger. I pestered my mum for them until she got sick of me asking and conceded. She really wanted me to learn the piano, so I made a compromise and agreed to learn that too.' She grinned. 'After a while I stopped having the lessons and basically taught myself.'

She shrugged, not wanting to make a big deal about her ability. Her reasons for learning to play both instruments had always been purely self-motivated. The plain truth of the matter was that her music and her books had kept her sane whenever life had threatened to get a little less dependable and reliable—like when her parents had announced they were leaving the country to join her brother Phil in America.

Phil was the 'blue-eyed boy' who, in their eyes, could do no wrong. An old familiar twinge of resentment surfaced but Caitlin quickly squashed it. At the time her sense of abandonment had been acute and music had been her only solace—an anchor in a world where nothing had made sense any more. She'd often wondered if that was why she had hooked up with someone like Sean. He'd entered her life when she'd been feeling especially low and he'd charmed her with his boyish smile, amusing jokes and the sense that he was a bit of rebel. She, poor fool, had lapped up his attention as though she'd been marooned on a desert island for years without seeing a single soul.

Mike was thoughtful. There was a real buzz of excitement in the pit of his belly when he thought about Caitlin and what she could potentially bring to the table for the band. Not only had they found themselves an amazing singer, but he'd discovered another musician he could harmonise with as well. There was no doubt in his mind that they could be a great team. The girl was worth her weight in gold.

'What you did just now was more than "good", Caitlin. You really know how to play.'

'Thanks.' Her smile was shy, but appreciative. After last night's humiliating little encounter with Jake as they were watching the band she definitely welcomed a boost to her morale this morning.

God, she'd made such a fool of herself. Her heart thudded and slowed at the memory. It had been a bad mistake to let him see how much she wanted him. *Not that she'd had much choice in the matter, when her body had seemed to have an agenda all of its own...*

But then afterwards, when he had dropped her home to her flat after a near silent car journey filled with the most electrifying tension, Jake had confused her yet again when he'd insisted on accompanying her to her door and waiting until she'd got safely inside. There had been no sign of his earlier rejection at the concert.

The man was a genuine enigma and no mistake. Yet Caitlin understood why he had to put the band first. He wouldn't jeopardise Blue Sky's chances by having a meaningless fling with their new lead singer. *Not that any association with Jake, however brief, could ever be meaningless...*

'Have you had the chance to learn the two new songs I gave you?' Mike asked, his glance flicking interestedly over the pretty white gypsy-style blouse she was wearing with faded blue jeans.

'After I got home from the gig I was up most of last night working on them,' Caitlin told him, suppressing a yawn. She carefully withdrew a folded sheet of paper from her jeans pocket. 'Do you want to give them a try?'

'Sure. That would be great.' Picking up his guitar again, Mike started to tune it.

The unexpected sound of a ring on the doorbell interrupted him and he broke off to spring nimbly to his feet. During his absence Caitlin took the opportunity to lean back against the edge of the pink velour couch behind her, stretch out her legs and idly finger her guitar strings. As much as she wanted and needed to learn the songs, it had probably not been the most sensible thing to do to stay up long into the early hours trying to master them. *What she wouldn't give for a long lie-down...*

Her eyes drifting closed, she was just wondering how on earth she was going to get through the rest of the day when the sense that she had company alerted her. She looked up to find Jake staring down at her. He had a disconcerting glint in his eye that made Caitlin shiver helplessly, and she hastily sat up to drape her arm protectively across her guitar. *What had she done wrong now?*

'Hi.' It wasn't easy to sound casual when all she could think about was what had happened between them at the gig. But straight away Jake was all business.

'You're giving rehearsals a miss this afternoon. We're going out,' he declared.

Dazedly, she answered, 'We are?'

Mike had come back into the room behind him and her gaze swung from his to Mike's and back again.

'Not Mike,' Jake qualified firmly. 'Just you and me. I'm taking you shopping.'

'But I don't want to go shopping.' Caitlin didn't even pause to wonder what for. All she knew was that she was in no fit condition to trudge round some overheated shopping mall—with or *without* Jake.

'This has got to be a first. A woman who doesn't like shopping? Where have you been all my life?' Mike joked.

But Jake didn't look remotely amused. His handsome countenance was as implacable as usual. In his black leather coat and blue jeans, his square jaw fashionably unshaven, he looked as if he was in no mood to entertain an argument, no matter how convincing or passionate. Caitlin tensed.

'Get your coat,' he ordered.

'But Mike and I were just—'

'I'm not interested. I just want you to get your coat and be quick about it. I don't want this to take any longer than it has to.'

He had a nerve! It was at Jake's suggestion the previous night that Caitlin had come round to Mike's to get some guitar practice in.

'You can't just walk in here and tell me what to do.' She defiantly stayed where she was, even though her heart was beating like a jackhammer. Blue Sky's lead guitarist was staring down at his feet as if they were suddenly the most interesting sight in the world. *No moral support there, she thought irritably.*

'I thought I'd just done exactly that.' Lifting a mocking eyebrow, Jake was unimpressed. 'Now, if you want to continue to be a member of this band, I'd seriously consider doing what you're told and being quick about it. We're driving to London, and at this rate we won't get there before one o'clock. That hardly gives us enough time.'

'Enough time for *what*?'

Clearly mad at him, Caitlin finally got to her feet, gripping her precious guitar by its neck as if it was Jake's neck she'd like to throttle. Her pretty face was flushed with emotion, her bewitching emerald eyes spitting fire, and in that instant Jake experienced a longing for her so deep that it hurt.

He knew he was only being short-tempered because he was furious with himself for wanting her so badly. Tough. Life could be unfair like that. If there had been the remotest possibility that they could find another singer even half as good as Caitlin, then he would seriously have considered letting her go. The band and Rick would undoubtedly give him hell but, damn it, if it was a choice between confronting their rage and losing his sanity then he knew which one he'd plump for.

The sheets on his bed had been a crumpled mess when he'd woken this morning. If he'd slept two hours he'd be surprised. It had been a hell of a long time since any woman had got Jake in such a stew—not since Jodie, and that had been six years ago. But even at the height of his attraction to Jodie it had never been like this. This mindless, helpless, heated longing that he felt for Caitlin was driving him slowly crazy.

If she had been any other woman but Blue Sky's new lead singer he wouldn't have hesitated in succumbing to his carnal desires. But Caitlin Ryan was strictly off-limits. *Hadn't he said so to himself when he'd first heard her sing?*

'Jake?' When he didn't immediately reply, but levelled his compelling blue gaze straight at her in warning, Caitlin had to suppress the worrying impulse to leave, to put herself out of the line of fire. Why was he so furious with her? What had she done to make him so disagreeable?

'You need some clothes,' he explained grudgingly. 'Working clothes. The band plays its first date in London next week and we need to kit you out. I've arranged to meet a stylist I've worked with for years…someone I trust who will help guide you. Her name is Ronnie. Rick has had to drive up north on business, so today's a good opportunity to sort things out. Now, go and get your coat…*please.*'

Driving a weary hand through his tousled mane, Jake looked as if his patience was being sorely tested. In the meantime, Caitlin's mind was racing. *He was taking her to buy clothes?* That would mean she'd have to parade herself in front of him, not to mention this stylist, whilst getting hot and bothered, trying on garments in cramped changing rooms and no doubt feeling woefully inadequate when something didn't look right or didn't fit.

Was it really necessary that he go with her? And did she really need a professional stylist to help her choose the right clothes? Couldn't Jake simply trust her own judgement as far as dressing herself went?

One look into that arrogant male visage and she had her answer. She could stand there and argue until they got old and Jake would still insist on going with her.

'I hate and detest shopping,' she said, before turning on her heel and grabbing her coat off the back of the pink velour armchair. 'And if you think for one second that I'm pouring myself into some horrible skin-tight catsuit for the sake of this band then you've got another think coming!'

And with that she shouldered angrily past Jake out into the hallway—but not before suffering the added indignity of hearing the two men she'd left behind chuckling between them in some ancient patronising ritual of amused male bonding.

CHAPTER SIX

JAKE COULDN'T REMEMBER the last time he'd had so much fun. Nor could he remember his inflamed libido being put under such torturous conditions in an even longer time. An obliging assistant—a skinny little redhead, with pansy-blue eyes and freckles—had thoughtfully supplied him with a comfy chair while Ronnie, the dependable stylist, selected several items of clothing from the rails and at regular intervals handed them to Caitlin to try on.

As she disappeared in and out of the changing room, trying on various different outfits, her expression veered alternately from plain put upon to seriously contemplating doing him some damage. The funny thing was, even when she was scowling at him, Caitlin was prettier and sexier than any other woman he could think of. So, although their little shopping trip had a serious purpose, it was also providing Jake with some royal entertainment.

'You didn't tell me this would be one of the easiest assignments you've ever given me, Jake. This girl is an absolute dream to dress!' The fashionable and gamine stylist curved her scarlet-painted lips with pleasure as she dropped down beside Jake. 'I mean, I've dressed some of the best female recording artists in the world, and all I can tell you is if she sings as good as she looks…'

'She does,' he assured her laconically. Then, with a sigh, he added, 'Whether you're a record producer or the manager of a band, singers like Caitlin come along once in a lifetime…*if* you're lucky.'

'Then one thing's for sure, my friend,' Ronnie said, knowingly patting his knee. 'The rest of the music industry will be quaking in their boots—because without a doubt this amazing find of yours is definitely going to put you back in the game...with bells on!'

And on that note, as if on cue, with an impatient swish of the changing room curtain Caitlin suddenly appeared before them wearing red faux leather jeans cut low on the hip and a sheer white chiffon blouse that had a lacy frill edging the cuffs. And, because the diaphanous blouse revealed so much more than it concealed, Jake was treated to the captivating sight of her luscious breasts crammed into a flimsy white lace bra that appeared barely equipped to contain them. He also saw that she had a deeply sexy belly button that put him in mind of a harem and long, hot desert nights...

With her arms akimbo, she glanced first at Ronnie, then at him, and her bewitching green eyes clearly proclaimed her disdain.

'I hope you're both satisfied. In my opinion, I look utterly ridiculous in this outfit.' Flicking back her shining dark hair in a huff, Caitlin flushed, her apple cheeks growing even pinker.

When Ronnie would have gone across to reassure her, Jake immediately rose to his feet to take charge.

'Let *me*,' he told her meaningfully, lowering his voice.

He made his way over to his new protégée.

'Believe me, you look anything *but* ridiculous.'

A heated injection of pure carnal pleasure pulsed through him as he came face to face with Caitlin's arrestingly beautiful gaze. His blood had been simmering since she had got into the car with him outside Mike's place and, as entertaining and necessary as it was, this little fashion parade wasn't helping.

Everything about the woman was driving him wild...her scent, her beautiful emerald eyes, that gorgeous long black hair of hers, and even the endearing little habit she had of chewing down on her lower lip when she was feeling over-whelmed or anxious. *As for her figure... Ever since he had seen it he'd been thanking God he was born a man.* It was a shame they were in one of his stylist's favourite fashion houses or he might have demonstrated his appreciation a little more graphically.

'Well, I'm not going on stage looking like this. I haven't become a singer for people to ogle me. If you like the outfit so much, why don't *you* wear it and be done with it!'

Caitlin stepped towards Jake as if she'd like to wipe the smile right off his face with a slap. Towering over her, he immediately closed the gap between them and made himself slowly breathe out.

'Calm down. You're getting all hot and bothered for nothing.'

Hot and bothered didn't begin to describe how Jake was feeling. God knew he was making a supreme effort to corral his aroused feelings, but it was damn near impossible with Caitlin huffing and pink-cheeked in front of him, her luscious breasts rising and falling with every breath that she took.

'Ronnie and I just wanted you to try a few different looks. It doesn't mean you have to go with anything that doesn't feel right. Ultimately it's your decision.'

Jake's reassurance effectively took the wind out of Caitlin's sails. She hadn't meant to be deliberately obstructive, but appearing in revealing clothing in front of *anyone,* let alone Jake, wasn't something that came remotely easy to her. It wasn't anyone's fault that she was so insecure about her body, but she *was.* She'd often been teased as a child for being 'chubby', and even though she knew rationally that she was in good shape now she guessed that the hurt of being picked on and singled out because of her appearance had never quite left her.

But maybe this was her chance to overcome her insecurities and act differently for once. In any case, the least she could do was have a sense of humour about the proceedings. The fact was, she was a singer in a rock band and people would expect her to look the part...even to look *sexy*.

Cringing at the thought, she suddenly found herself unable to meet Jake's glance directly. He was so arresting, from the top of his tousled dark hair and the haunting chiselled perfection of his face to the tips of his feet in his stylish worn leather boots. In his long leather coat, with tight jeans and a midnight-blue shirt opened casually at the neck, he wore his clothes as if he didn't give a damn...which made it all the more challenging for Caitlin, knowing she regularly had to face him.

'I don't like wearing this kind of revealing clothing. I'm just not comfortable dressing to show off my body,' she admitted quietly. And because she was feeling vulnerable, every cell vibrating with the tension of being so intimately scrutinised, she folded her arms across her chest, only too aware that Jake's heated blue gaze kept dipping helplessly to that area.

'Why?' Nonplussed, he shook his head. 'Tell me what's going on in your head that makes you feel embarrassed about revealing such a God-given asset? Because that's what it is, Caitlin.'

His glance momentarily flicked towards the elegant and manicured Ronnie, who sat waiting patiently for him to finish before coming over to join them and give her opinion.

'It's not easy to explain,' Caitlin answered.

Jake turned back to her to give her his full attention. Taking up where he'd left off, he remarked, 'You're beautiful, Caitlin. If I gave you a bin liner to wear you'd still look stunning. Why don't you just enjoy being young, having the freedom to dress a little outrageously?'

'It's all right for a man to come out with that, isn't it?' Furiously twining her hair behind her ear, Caitlin glared. 'Women don't leave men just because they get older. Even nowadays, when you'd think we would have got a little bit more enlightened, older men are labelled "interesting" or "experienced" while the complete reverse is applied to women.'

An amused smile twitched at the corners of Jake's lips.

Caitlin paused. Maybe she was overreacting. After all, surely he had a point—she should take advantage of being young and free and go wild. Still, his sentiment had struck a nerve. Was Jake the kind of man who would leave a woman just because she was getting older or had put on weight? The music industry was hardly known for nurturing healthy relationships, was it? Not when everything seemed to be dominated by image these days.

The pop charts were littered with pretty young things with average talent and attractive bodies who had their five minutes of fame and then disappeared. But, as far as relationships went, it didn't mean that she couldn't fantasise about one day finding a man who wanted to stay with her come what may. It was just a shame that Jake Sorenson clearly *wasn't* and never could be that man. He might be attracted to her because he admired the 'packaging', but that was all it was: a passing meaningless attraction that would no doubt blow itself out as soon as he'd taken her to bed... *if she let him.*

The thought made her heart slam against her ribs.

'Don't paint all us men with the same brush.' Reaching out his hand, Jake gently loosed the glossy strand of hair that Caitlin had tucked behind her ear and watched it glance against her cheek as it fell silkily down to her shoulder. 'I sincerely hope I'm not as shallow as you seem to think I am. When you get past the physical attraction, I'm quite aware there's got to be something deeper and more compelling to keep both parties in a relationship interested. If I found a woman I wanted to spend the rest of my life with I'd never let her go...no matter what happened.'

Jake's arresting blue eyes were regarding her so intently that Caitlin felt the imprint of his gaze resonate deep inside her. Along with the heartfelt words he'd expressed, his intensely examining glance shook and unravelled her. It made her body burn and her heart race. It stirred a longing in her for things that she knew could never be.

'This is the last outfit Ronnie gave me to try on. I think I'll go and get changed now. I suddenly feel quite cold.'

Despite the intimacy that Jake had woven round them, the harsh cold reality of the situation suddenly doused the heat that had all but drowned her just a moment ago. *Caitlin was beginning to care too much for Jake and that was dangerous.*

Turning away, she rubbed briskly at the chilled flesh on her arms in the diaphanous blouse, and was taken aback when he moved swiftly behind her and turned her firmly back round to face him.

'That first outfit you tried on…the purple velvet top and the long black skirt with the chain belt? That looked great. Shall we go with that for starters?'

A muscle flexed in the side of his lean jaw. The outfit he'd described was one of her favourites, too. *It seemed that they agreed on something after all.*

'Okay.'

'And, by the way, we're not going straight home after this. We're going back to Ronnie's place for a while, then I'm taking you to a club. We'll eat dinner there and enjoy some entertainment.'

He was taking her to a club? What was that all about?

'Why didn't you mention this before? What kind of club?'

Jake's expression remained as inscrutable as ever, yet he definitely had a twinkle in his eye. Caitlin frowned. *What on earth was the man up to?*

'I wanted it to be a surprise,' he drawled. 'Hopefully an enjoyable one.'

'I've hardly got the right clothes with me to go out for the evening…especially to a club. Can't we leave it for another night?'

Ignoring her hopeful plea, he clenched his jaw and firmly shook his head.

'Sorry, but you're not going to wriggle out of this one. Trust me. Tonight will be just what you need. As for not having the right clothes—why don't you pick out one of the outfits you were looking at to wear? You can get ready at Ronnie's.'

'Those outfits are ludicrously expensive, Jake! I can't afford—'

'I'm footing the bill. You can have anything you like—and I mean anything. Think of it as a gift.'

More than a little overwhelmed by his unexpected generosity, she was almost lost for words. 'Well…I mean, that's very kind of you, but just what kind of place is this club you're taking me to?'

He smiled one of his maddening sexy smiles that could stop a woman in her tracks in less than a heartbeat and said, 'It's classy…very classy. That's all you need to know.'

'Let me help you to choose something. Jake has told me where you'll be going and I know the perfect outfit. We'll also need to accessorise you with shoes and jewellery to complete the look.'

The fragrant Ronnie was suddenly at her side and, whilst Caitlin had plenty of reservations about being kitted out for an evening out with Jake somewhere 'classy', she sensed that any more attempts at wriggling out of the night's events would be a waste of energy.

In the sumptuous mirrored enclave of the exclusive members-only jazz club, frequented not just by aficionados but by many well-known celebrities from the worlds of music and film, Jake sat opposite Caitlin at a beautifully laid dining table and thanked the gods for giving him a legitimate excuse simply to sit and gaze at her.

Ronnie had helped select the perfect outfit for her tonight. The powers of the 'little black dress' should never be underestimated, she'd told him knowledgeably, and she'd been right. The slinky little number she'd come up with had taken his breath away when he'd seen Caitlin wearing it. It had a daringly low-cut neckline that immediately drew the eye to her sensational cleavage, and the fitted black satin clung to her body in all the right places. The voluptuous curves that she contrived to keep hidden from the world were tonight displayed in all their glory.

Add to that some sexy red lipstick and the sultry, alluring perfume that Jake had chosen especially for her—*he'd slipped out to purchase it as Caitlin had got dressed*—and he doubted there was a single male in the vicinity who would ever forget seeing her.

He sucked in some air and breathed it out again slowly. An unexpected need to protect her had crept into his blood and he couldn't help now and again surveying the other diners in case they looked a little *too* interested in her. He knew it was crazy when very soon Caitlin would be appearing with the band and from then on would be in the public domain. But in light of his protective feelings and undeniable need to keep her to himself, how was he going to handle it? he wondered. *It was a dilemma that had never affected him before...*

The manager of the venue—an immaculately dressed Frenchman called Dion, who famously took great pride in entertaining an elite clientele—had expressed delight at seeing Jake. It had been a long time since the two men had met. The last occasion had been just before his ex had written that dreadful exposé about him. After that Jake had retreated to lick his wounds and kept a deliberately low profile. Even so, the Frenchman had recognised Jake straight away.

'It's so nice to see you back in public again, Mr Sorenson,' he'd told him. 'It's been too long.' Then he'd turned to Caitlin and commented, 'Many beautiful women come to this establishment, but *you ma chère*...you take my breath away!'

In truth, Jake had almost been readying himself for a small stampede when he'd walked in with Caitlin on his arm. He'd honestly sensed the moment when the other stylishly attired patrons seated at the tables had drawn in a collective awed breath. They might be surprised at seeing him out in public again, but he doubted their interest was solely in him. The woman by his side was the main reason they glanced their way, and Jake would be a liar if he didn't admit to feeling both pride and pleasure at the realisation. After all, he was only human.

Although the club featured predominantly jazz, and there was a smoky-sounding sax playing in the background, tonight was Burlesque night,—and that was what he'd brought Caitlin to see.

'This is some place,' she commented shyly.

'And you've just elevated it to a whole other class,' he said, and smiled.

Delicately sipping her Margarita, she added, 'I feel so guilty drinking this when you're just drinking soda and lime.'

'There's no need. I'm quite happy being teetotal tonight. Especially when I have a very precious cargo to drive home,' he teased.

Jake supposed it was inevitable that the compliment would make her cheeks turn pink, but he loved to see her blush. It reminded him that she was still relatively innocent...*quite a rarity in his world.*

'I've heard of Burlesque, but I don't know very much about it. Isn't it some kind of variety show?' she enquired.

Even before he told her the answer Jake sensed the muscles in his belly clench hard in anticipation of her reaction.

'It can be that. But Burlesque is really an art form...it's about celebrating the beauty of the female form.'

'Oh...? You mean it involves things like striptease?'

'It's much more than women simply taking their clothes off. Sometimes all a girl might remove are her gloves. But it's the way they do it that makes it an art form. Plus the costumes the girls wear and the way they move is part of the spectacle. I just want you to sit back and enjoy it...to feel proud of being a woman.'

'Is that why you brought me here? To show me how women can be confident about displaying their bodies when they perform? So I won't be self-conscious when I perform with the band?'

'Yes. You're already going to command the stage with that incredible voice of yours, but I don't want any doubts about your body to hold you back. I want you to enjoy every second you're on that stage when you perform.'

To his surprise, Caitlin downed what was left of her cocktail with a flourish, licked her lips and declared, 'In that case I think I'd like another drink...a little Dutch courage wouldn't go amiss. Do you mind?'

'Are you serious?' Leaning over to her, Jake tenderly stroked the pad of his thumb down over her cheek and said huskily, 'Baby, do you have *any* idea how dangerously alluring you are in that dress? If you asked me to get you the moon I'd do my damnedest to get it for you.'

'Oh, I wouldn't expect you to go *that* far,' she said, and grinned.

His lips twitching in amusement and delight, because Caitlin was clearly starting to enjoy herself, Jake signalled for a waitress to take his order just as the sultry sax in the background came to a sudden halt, the lights dimmed and all eyes turned expectantly towards the stage...

The show was spectacular. Caitlin was swept away by the sumptuous display of dance and movement from the predominantly 'Rubenesque' women who took to the stage in their stunning costumes and exaggerated make-up. At no point did she feel remotely embarrassed or self-conscious at all the comely flesh on display. For perhaps the very first time she felt proud to be a woman and unashamed of her own voluptuous curves.

Jake had been right. It had been a good idea to bring her to a Burlesque night. *But her companion hadn't reserved*

all his attention for the show. More than once throughout
the evening she'd caught him looking at her as though mesmerised, despite having a bevy of stunning women on the
stage in front of them.

*That brooding glance of his had made Caitlin feel more
than a little aroused. In fact it had made her long for him
to take her somewhere private so that she could demonstrate exactly just how excited he made her feel...* And Jake
wasn't the only one who was enjoying the view. Dressed in
the flawless single-breasted Armani suit that unbeknownst
to her he'd brought with him to change into for their visit
to the club, with his incredible blue eyes glinting like dia-
monds and his chiselled jaw dusted with late-night shadow,
he looked expensive and assured, and he exuded the kind of
charisma usually attributed to A-list movie stars.

Caitlin wanted to pinch herself to make sure she wasn't
dreaming that he was solely hers for the evening. Who would
have guessed that a man who famously adopted a 'don't give
a damn' attitude about what he was wearing could wear a
tux with such effortless panache?

Later that night, as Jake turned the Jeep onto the motor-
way to head home, he wondered wryly if Caitlin had any
idea what a test it was for him to concentrate on his driving when she was snuggled in the seat next to him wearing
that alluring black dress. The 'LBD', as Ronnie had called
it, had put him in a state of highly charged sexual tension
for the whole evening, and he knew it wasn't going to dis-
sipate easily.

By the time they'd reached the village and Jake had pulled
up outside Caitlin's flat he was honestly glad of the opportunity to get a breath of fresh air to help him think straight.
But first he had to wake her and help her to the door, because she'd fallen asleep as soon as they'd got into the car.
It was inevitable she would be a little drowsy.

'Hey, sleepyhead, we're home.'

Curling his hand round her slim upper arm, Jake shook

her gently. The second she opened her big green eyes the tension that already gripped him mercilessly doubled.

'Have I been asleep? I must have been, because that journey went in a blink.'

Shaking her head, Caitlin undid her seatbelt and sat up. Her lustrous dark hair spilled down over her shoulders and the air was suddenly provocatively imbued with the sultry scent Jake had bought her. *What had he been trying to do? Make her even more irresistible than she was already?*

'Well, we're home now, and you need to get straight to bed,' he stated, almost groaning out loud at his ill thought out choice of words—because that was *exactly* where he'd like to go with her. 'Give me your key. I'll open the door for you,' he added.

The cold night air hit him as soon as he stepped out of the car and proved to be just the tonic he needed to cool his blood. Quickly inserting Caitlin's key into the lock, he opened the door onto the hallway and waited for her to step over the threshold in front of him. As soon as she did Jake's blood was stirred all over again when she turned back towards him. She'd draped her jacket over her shoulders and now tugged the sides more closely over her chest, but not before he had a glimpse of her delectable cleavage. *For both their sakes he should say goodnight and leave her.* His usually dependable sense of control was rapidly deserting him.

But his decision was immediately compromised when Caitlin narrowed the gap between them and said softly, 'Thanks for a really wonderful evening, Jake, and also for the lovely clothes and everything. You made me feel like a princess, and no one's ever done that for me before.'

'It wasn't difficult, Caitlin. In my eyes you *are* a princess.'

It was then that Jake thought, *To hell with self-control* and pulled her into his arms. He kissed her with a hunger he could no longer deny, and the desire that was always just a breath away whenever they were together flared beyond control. But when Caitlin carefully freed her lips and he saw the longing in her eyes—*the kind of longing that went way beyond a desire simply to make love*—the immensity of what he was contemplating and the possible consequences hit him like a brick dropped from a great height.

With his heart thundering, Jake moved out of their embrace. 'I think it's time we said goodnight, don't you? It's been a long day for both of us and we're just a couple of days away from the band's first live performance. We need to get some rest to make sure we're fit for what's to come.'

'I know you're right, but—'

Even before Caitlin had finished what she was saying Jake was out through the door and walking towards the car.

Two days of intense rehearsal followed Caitlin's magical night out with Jake. And, although she'd had a wonderful time, she couldn't forget how quickly he'd distanced himself from her after he'd dropped her home—even though just before he'd left, his lips had passionately claimed hers as if he really meant it. Now he was acting as if the kiss had never even happened. It was easy to sense that his focus was back on the band and what lay ahead of them, but Caitlin couldn't help feeling he was somehow abandoning her.

A couple of evenings later Jake surprised them all by giving them a day off. They'd had two more gruelling days of rehearsal and they more than welcomed the unexpected opportunity for a bit of 'R&R'. But, although Caitlin appreciated being able to rest and have a day to herself, she started to fret about the upcoming live shows. The new-found confidence she'd experienced after seeing the Burlesque seemed to be rapidly diminishing.

Having the day off hadn't helped. All it had done was to make her worry even more. That was why she found herself making her way to the Pilgrim's Inn that night, hopefully to see Jake and express her concerns. Just a few dedicated patrons occupied the cosily lit lounge bar and Caitlin was grateful, because it had taken every ounce of courage she could muster to make this eleventh hour trip to speak with Jake.

As far as Blue Sky's enigmatic manager was concerned his new lead singer would be having an early night and dreaming about what a resounding success she was going to be when she debuted with the band—because tomorrow was the big day: the day when Blue Sky introduced their new female vocalist to the world…or at least to the audience at the famous rock café in London where they were playing.

But Caitlin wasn't just apprehensive about what lay ahead, she was plain *petrified*—so petrified that she was suddenly having some serious doubts.

I'm sorry but I've made a terrible mistake. She heard the words go round and round in her head and imagined the confusion and then anger in Jake's eyes when she said them.

She sighed. *She didn't really want to quit.* All she was looking for was a little reassurance. If Jake couldn't give it to her, after all his years of experience in working with singers and musicians, she didn't have a prayer.

Tina Stevens was busy polishing the bar, her jaw working overtime as she chewed on some gum, her long red nails clicking against the varnished wood as she ran a duster over the already shiny surface of the counter. The brown eyes that were heavily outlined with kohl gave Caitlin a cool once-over as she approached, but she continued to polish as though her life depended on it.

'Excuse me, I—'

'What can I get you, love? Are you on your own or are you meeting somebody?'

There was a distinct note of disapproval in the blonde's voice, as if she believed that women who came into bars on their own somehow spelt trouble.

For a disconcerting moment Caitlin wondered if Tina had been working that night when Sean had turned particularly nasty. But, unable to remember very much other than the soul-destroying humiliation of being insulted by her boyfriend in public, she opted not to dwell on it. *Goodness knew she had enough on her mind without fretting about the past.* All she wanted—all she needed—was for Jake to tell her that everything would be all right, that she wasn't about to suffer another humiliation tomorrow night when she sang.

'I'm not meeting anybody.' Pushing her rain-dampened fringe out of her eyes, she squared her shoulders in her long charcoal-coloured raincoat. 'I wondered if I could have a word with Jake Sorenson? He's staying here, isn't he?'

Immediately Tina stopped polishing, and her expression was far from convivial. As the two women faced each other the record that was playing on the juke box suddenly changed and a song that Caitlin remembered from her childhood replaced it. *It was her mother's favourite song.*

An avid music fan, Terry Ryan had played the tune to death when Caitlin was little. She would enfold her little daughter in her arms and dance round the room with her, crooning gently against her cheek as she softly sang the words, whilst Phil—Caitlin's older brother—who was disdainful of anything remotely 'girly' would groan in mockery.

'Typical boy!' her mother would say, and laugh, instantly forgiving him as though it was his birthright.

Memories... Caitlin suddenly found herself pole-axed by them. Treacherously, her eyes filled with tears. What was *wrong* with her?

She was missing her family—that was what was wrong. Here she was, on the eve of what could be one of the most important nights of her life, and where were her parents and brother? On the other side of the world! They were completely oblivious to the fact that Caitlin had resigned from her job, never mind joined a rock band as their lead singer!

She had never felt as alone or as afraid as she did right then. She was twenty-six years old, about to embark on the biggest challenge she could imagine, with nothing but her dreams, her wits and her talent to help see her through.

'You must be Cait...the singer.'

As if it had suddenly dawned on her who Caitlin was, Tina stopped chewing her gum and crossed her arms in front of her chest. The sudden movement jiggled her ample breasts in the red V-necked angora sweater she wore. Well… *nearly* wore.

'It's Caitlin.' The correction of her name was automatic. She remembered that Rick had been using the shortened version of it since he'd met her, and that he apparently had a real soft spot for the buxom Miss Stevens.

'Yeah…right. All set for tomorrow, then?' the other girl asked.

Not really.

'I hope so. Could I see Jake?' Caitlin's lip quivered a little as she made an attempt at a friendly smile.

'Room Three. Turn left at the top of the stairs.'

'Thanks.'

'Nice talking to you.'

Could have fooled me, Caitlin thought.

Making her way up the thickly carpeted staircase, with its faded floral tread, she focused her gaze on the landing at the top, on the ponderous oak sideboard with its gaudy Victorian lamp and the sepia-toned photographs of the village that were displayed on the wall behind it.

The dark old-fashioned surroundings seemed incongruous when she thought of Jake. She wondered why he hadn't rented a house in the village, like the other band members had. But then it occurred to her that maybe Rick had something to do with his decision to stay at the Pilgrim's Inn. Perhaps the voluptuous Tina Stevens had an equally arresting friend he wanted to introduce to Jake, for instance?

Disliking that particular train of thought, Caitlin arrived at the top of the stairs and glanced anxiously round her. Two doors faced each other across the landing. Before she could talk herself out of it she rapped briskly on number three. She immediately registered the sound of male voices coming from the room and realised that Jake and Rick must be in conference about the concert tomorrow.

She didn't know whether to stay put or turn around and leave. But the decision was made for her when the door suddenly opened and Rick appeared. Untypically, when his usual mode of dress was more extrovert, he was wearing a pair of ordinary faded Levi's and a plain white T-shirt.

He gave Caitlin his trademark roguish smile when he saw that it was her. 'Hello, gorgeous. Come to join the party?'

His candid gaze moved over her figure in her buttoned-up raincoat—possibly the most unsexy item of clothing she possessed. But Caitlin didn't give the thought much attention.

'No. I mean, I just came to see Jake…if I could?'

Her mouth suddenly drying, she stared across the top of Rick's hard-muscled shoulder and found the man she was looking for. His long-legged form was lounging in an overstuffed green and gold striped armchair and his glance met hers, a knowing smile curving his lips. *He looked as if he'd been expecting her visit.*

Her feverish thoughts went into overdrive. He'd given them all the day off and advised them to get an early night in preparation for the following day, but he clearly didn't apply the advice to himself. Did the man *ever* get an early night in his business? Caitlin somehow doubted it.

'If I've come at a bad time—' she started, suddenly embarrassed. Had any of his other artists ever sought him out the night before a debut concert to seek his reassurance she wondered? Would her sudden attack of nerves disturb him and make him doubt his decision to hire her as Marcie's replacement?

He must have intuited that she was on the point of changing her mind about talking to him because he said suddenly, 'Stay right where you are.'

The words were uttered like a command from on high and Caitlin immediately froze. Rick sighed and moved away as Jake took a couple of leisurely strides towards her. As he drew near she saw that his hard, lean jaw was dark with late-night shadow and his slightly cool stare put her on her guard. That less than friendly glance hardly invited a frank admission about her doubts and feelings concerning the gig tomorrow, she thought anxiously.

'I thought you might come to see me tonight,' he drawled.

'Did you?' Caitlin heard the strength in her voice desert her.

'Yes, I did' He turned round to find Rick. 'Give us a few minutes, will you? Come to think of it, we'll probably need a little longer than that. Go and have a drink with Tina.'

Looking doubtful, his colleague shrugged. 'I'd really like to oblige, Jake, but whether Miss Cold-as-Ice down there will even serve me is another matter. We've had a bit of a falling out.'

'You brought it on yourself, Rick. Sort it out.'

'Sure. You're the boss.'

Clearly unhappy, Rick didn't say another word. But he still found a smile for Caitlin as he passed her. Then he left the room, shutting the door firmly behind him. She shivered. She suddenly didn't feel at all easy about finding herself alone with Jake.

'Can I get you a drink?' The charismatic manager strolled across to another ponderous Victorian sideboard and, opening a door, extracted a bottle of Bourbon along with two glasses.

'No. Not for me, thanks.'

When Caitlin declined his offer without further ado he poured himself a conservative amount of alcohol into a shot glass and advanced slowly towards her. Not for a second did he take his glance off her. His blue eyes glinted dangerously, just like a shaft of sunlight catching the burnished blade of a sword. She couldn't help tensing. *The charming man in the Armani tux who had taken her to the Burlesque had apparently disappeared.*

Tipping back his glass, Jake swallowed down the drink

before saying, 'So…care to tell me why you've come to see me tonight, Caitlin? It certainly isn't to make small talk, is it? What's on your mind? In my experience there's only *one* reason a woman comes to a man's hotel room late at night.'

As if to illustrate what he meant, he flicked his intense gaze over her as if he'd like to strip every stitch from her body and devour her, and then take his slow, sweet time doing it all over again.

Caitlin tried desperately to calm the rioting sensations he was stirring inside her.

'Well, that's not the reason I came to see you, Jake… as hard as that might be for your ego to take. My visit is a purely practical one.'

'Is it?' His expression doubtful, he put his glass down on a nearby side table and turned back to give her a deliberately lazy smile. 'You break my heart, Caitlin Ryan…but I think you know that, don't you?'

'What do you mean?'

Her mind was in a complete spin, and if she hadn't backed herself up against the door just then there was a distinct danger that she might simply have crumpled to the floor. Her legs were trembling so hard they hardly seemed to have the strength to keep her upright.

'What you do to me with those slow, hot looks of yours is nothing less than criminal.'

His voice a low, grating rasp, Jake yanked her away from the door and pulled her roughly into his arms.

CHAPTER SEVEN

CRIMINAL... CAITLIN COULD have used the same adjective to describe Jake's kiss. The way he took her mouth was near savage, and it almost knocked her off of her feet. This was no inept fumbling, no tentative exploration, but a devastating passionate assault on the senses.

With a hungry groan that seemed to emanate from the depths of his soul, he swept his tongue over the warm recesses of her surprised mouth as one firm hand possessively anchored itself in the long thick strands of her hair to render the contact between them even more intimate.

As his tongue thrust deeper, harder, mimicking the ultimate sexual coupling between a man and a woman, Caitlin swallowed her breath, tasting him, her senses intoxicated by the dark sultry flavours of bourbon and avaricious heat. She gripped onto the sensuous silk of his shirt with all the strength and tenacity of someone hanging from a precipice by their fingertips...as if she dangled into empty space and could fall at any moment.

But from the instant Jake had captured her mouth there had been no thought to deny him. Not when everything in her clamoured wildly for more of the same. Only a frigid woman could not want what Jake was giving her right now, and Caitlin was anything but that. She was a living, breathing, loving human being, and it was too long since she'd been held and desired—too long since she'd been loved like a woman longed to be loved by a man.

Oh God...how did I survive without this? she thought.

All she knew was that her legs suddenly didn't have a hope of holding her up for very much longer. Not when the equivalent of a hundred volts of pure unadulterated pleasure was pulsating through her as though she were plugged in to her own personal ecstasy machine.

Almost mindlessly driving her hips against Jake's, she heard herself moaning urgent little sounds of want and need—sounds that were as alien to her as this wild, savage joy that was pouring through her veins. Sean had never taken her anywhere *near* close to the kind of heights Jake was taking her to now. Never before had passion come at her like a wild, untamed river, bursting its banks, sweeping everything that stood in its way to exciting unchartered shores that left her dazed and trembling.

Hungrily she acquiesced as he alternately nipped and grazed at her mouth, every now and then her tongue meeting and dancing with his, her breasts burning into the hard granite wall of his chest. She was certain of one thing and one thing only...that she never wanted this sweet, irresistible agony to end.

Unbelievably, Jake turned up the heat. Now their invisible passion dial hovered somewhere between boiling and the point of no return. As he rocked his hips deep into hers the solid ridge of his button fly was testimony to his driving, hungry need, and when he suddenly broke contact to look down at her Caitlin glanced back at him in surprise.

It was a shock to witness the depth and strength of desire contained in that blistering gaze. His pupils were almost totally black, ringed with just the slimmest band of devastating blue. From his lips his breath issued hard and fast, and there was a thin sheen of sweat on his ridged brow.

'I don't want our first time to be up against a door. You've got to tell me what you want, baby.'

As he finished speaking he reached behind him and shot

the bolt, enveloping her in a dizzying cloak of heat and his disturbing, sensuous male essence.

'Do you want to stay with me tonight? We can go to bed now and finish what we started. I can keep you up all night and give you pleasure like you've never dreamed. Is that what you want?'

With deft fingers Jake freed the top three buttons on her coat and jerked the material aside to cup her breast through the thin material of her T-shirt. Her nipple, already rigid and tingling with need, pressed helplessly, wantonly into his palm.

Why did he have to stop and ask what she wanted? Caitlin thought. Why couldn't he just carry on the way they were going and take what she was so ready to give him?

She was shocked at the desperation of her wild thoughts. What he was doing—his long fingers now circling the nipple of her other breast, alternately nipping and squeezing—was making her womb throb with an almost unholy ache. If he took her right now she'd welcome the possession and count herself blessed. *That was how much she wanted him.* She was hungry to feel his sex deep inside her, to complete the electrifying bond that had been slowly and devastatingly drawing them together since the very first moment they had met.

But this was crazy—and not just crazy, but completely and utterly reckless. Jake must surely know that? He was the one who'd sternly advised Caitlin against 'fraternising' with the band out of hours, and as he was their manager he had to include himself in that warning. The potential pitfalls of turning a working relationship into a personal one could only spell disaster.

And, anyway, it was wrong to assume that Jake even *wanted* a personal relationship with her. A hot and fast seduction in a hotel room didn't usually pave the way to something deeper and more meaningful, did it? Was sex all that he wanted from her? If it was, then it was nothing less than an insult—because she was sure he could get that from any woman.

Realising how close she had come to throwing away something precious—namely her self-respect—Caitlin flung Jake's hand away and straightened her T-shirt. As she did so her heartbeat accelerated so hard she was momentarily dizzy. Seeing the spasm of confusion in his eyes, she sensed tension of another kind radiating from his body.

'What's wrong?' he ground out.

'I'm not going to sleep with you, Jake.'

'Sleeping isn't exactly what I had in mind.'

His words made her flinch. Her body hadn't stopped aching for him, and her mouth throbbed and burned from his unbelievably passionate kisses, but the idea that he would bed her simply just to 'scratch an itch' hurt her deeply. Having already had the soul-destroying experience of being used by a man, she wasn't about to set herself up to play the same old destructive tape again...

'All right, then, let me put it this way.' Impatiently she pushed back a drifting strand of hair from the side of her face to unwaveringly meet his gaze. 'I'm not going to have sex with you. I won't jeopardise my relationship with the band and neither will I be used by you because I happen to be "convenient". And, contrary to what you might believe, I didn't come here tonight because I had something personal in mind. All I wanted was a little reassurance because I was nervous about the performance tomorrow.'

Jake cursed softly beneath his breath. His disturbing blue eyes raked over her features, pinning her to the spot. It was clear to Caitlin that he was immersed in a deep inner tussle between utilising his common sense and trying to curtail his desire. Like her, he was still reeling from the throes of the incendiary passion they'd ignited. There was a thin film of sweat on his brow and it was evident he was still turned on. With the fulfilment of his desire evidently thwarted, now he was frustrated and angry as well as aroused.

'Is that what you think? That I'd take advantage and use you just because I wanted sex?' A muscle flexed warningly in the side of his exquisitely carved cheekbone. 'If you think that then I seriously underestimated you, Caitlin. You've listened to all the less than flattering stories about me, bought them as fact, and condemned me even though I told you the truth about what happened between me and my ex. Don't you remember that it was *my* reputation that got dragged through the mud because of the lies she wrote in that blasted article? *Not* hers?'

Caitlin hardly knew what to say. Was she guilty of judging Jake without trial? Without even giving him the chance to prove his character? After all, it wasn't just him that had suddenly found himself driven by the libidinous desires of the body. She was in exactly the same position!

Sighing, he agitatedly drove through his fingers through his already mussed hair.

'Anyway, perhaps you'd better just leave before my "questionable" character contaminates you even more. You'd better get home and get some rest. You know what's ahead of you tomorrow and I want you to be at your best.'

Her heart almost thudded to a stop. Tomorrow *would* be a big day…perhaps the most important one of her life so far. It was a shame that she'd spoiled things by coming over to Jake's and starting something she couldn't finish.

'I'm sorry that I—that I…'

'Don't beat yourself up about it. You're going to be just fine, Caitlin. That's what you want to know, isn't it? All you have to do is concentrate on the songs, the music. Blue Sky is a great band and they'll be helping you every step of the way. It's not going to be as hard as you imagine. Trust me. You've got a great voice and you're a stunning-looking girl. In terms of fulfilling the criteria for success in this business, you've got it all. You can't fail.'

If Jake had meant to reassure her he'd done it in a strangely reticent way. Caitlin still felt ill at ease. Plus she could easily sense the anger that simmered beneath his thin veneer of civility.

'I was going to say that I was sorry for—' Blushing, she was unable to complete the sentence when he was all but eating her up with his eyes.

'Turning me on?'

'I think I should go.'

'As much as it pains me to agree with you, you're probably right. Though that doesn't mean I wish you weren't.'

His words taunted her as Caitlin turned and fumbled with the bolt on the door. Then she fled from the room with a breathless 'goodnight' before she could change her mind.

Right then it was tempting for Jake to search for solace in the bottle of bourbon he had opened, but he couldn't fool himself that it would help. He'd been through enough heartache in his life already to think that it would.

His ex's wasn't the only betrayal he had endured. His mother had given him up for adoption when she'd found herself pregnant at just sixteen, and the home where she had placed Jake hadn't been able to find him adoptive parents due to his having a heart murmur. He had been in and out of hospital from birth up until he was eight years old for regular check-ups, by which time he had become quite used to being a bit of a loner. As he'd grown up and become stronger physically the heart murmur had corrected itself and he had resigned himself to living in the children's home until he reached sixteen.

Jake hadn't viewed it as a negative thing because by necessity it had taught him to be self-reliant. *The only friends he had depended on had been his books.* He had developed an insatiable curiosity about the world and had genuinely enjoyed reading and studying. Having done well in his exams, he'd managed to get himself a place at college, and then he'd found himself at university, studying cultural anthropology.

It was during that time that he had also developed an abiding interest in music. Jake's time at college and university had been his saving grace—along with a couple of genuinely caring and interested tutors who had encouraged him to go for his dreams and never to give them up.

Now, he stalked across the thickly carpeted floor and threw open the window onto the night. He was definitely in need of some fresh air. A fierce gust of wind hit him straight in the face, startling him, but it didn't remotely leech any of the heat from his body. *He knew himself to be too far gone for that.*

Even though Caitlin had left, he still burned from their passionate embrace. It was as though every nerve in his body throbbed with electricity and tension. Taking a cold shower was the obvious answer to try and ease his discomfort—but, frankly, it would be like putting a plaster on a third-degree burn. No...Jake would just have to wait it out. At least that or wait for some degree of common sense to return.

Caitlin Ryan had turned his whole world upside down. Here they were, at the start of the band's tour, and he had fallen like a ton of bricks for their new lead singer. He wouldn't go so far as to fool himself that he was in love with her—more *in lust*—but he was aware that one or two quick hot tumbles in bed were never going to be enough to satisfy the bone-deep yearning he had developed for her. Not for one moment had he meant for such a thing to happen, but somehow, in some way, Caitlin had got into Jake's blood and there wasn't much he could do about it.

How in hell was he supposed to keep a clear head and do all the things he normally had to do to help support and motivate the band? Get them out on the road with all guns blazing? Just seeing her every night for the next six weeks up on stage was going to be the sweetest torture. He already had to feel sorry for Rick and the others, because his mood sure as hell wasn't going to improve if he couldn't touch Caitlin in the way he ached to touch her. He'd either end up having to take religious vows or quit managing the band. Either way, his libido was definitely going to come under some serious duress.

The first shock Caitlin had received on reaching London was the discovery that she was going to be put up in Jake's flat in Chelsea for the two nights they were there. It had turned out that the rest of the band all had homes in the capital, including Rick. But Jake had quickly vetoed his friend's suggestion that Caitlin stay with him.

It had been too late for her to protest at the arrangement and organise an alternative, so she'd kept her doubts to herself and agreed. The most important thing was the coming performance, and she absolutely had to make a good impression...for *all* their sakes. But when they'd arrived at the fairly compact popular West London venue, Caitlin had found herself having to change into her stage gear in the ladies' room, because by the time they'd rehearsed, done a sound-check and had a meeting with the venue manager there had been no time to go back to Jake's place and get ready.

Frowning into one of the less than pristine mirrors, she had applied her make-up with a thumping heart and trembling hand, inadvertently spilling the contents of her make-up bag into the porcelain sink when she'd yanked out a tissue too hard to pat her lipstick dry with.

Now she stood in the wings with the rest of the band, feeling a bit like a little girl playing dress-up in her mother's best clothes, only partially tuning in to Rick's animated pep talk as he paced up and down in front of them, like an army sergeant pumping up his platoon for battle. In front of the small raised stage the crowd had swelled and the anticipation that crackled in the air was not dissimilar to the lightning strike before a torrential downpour.

There was a rumour going round that many of Blue Sky's fans who had supported them from the beginning with Marcie had turned up to support the band's return, in spite of their disappointment that she had walked out. Naturally Caitlin fretted that she would never pass muster.

Rick had told her that her style was quite different from Marcie's but that that was a *good* thing. Her strong vocal suited the band's music perfectly. *Like a match made in heaven,* he had assured her with a smile. But, while she welcomed the compliment, and was glad that the relative intimacy of the venue was perhaps not as intimidating as a much larger one might have been, her stomach was sick with nerves at the thought of being put through the ultimate baptism of fire for a new singer.

And where was Jake? He had been with them up until about half an hour ago, when he'd murmured something about 'last-minute arrangements' then disappeared. Caitlin found that now, when it came to the crunch, she needed his assurance more than ever.

'Is everyone okay?'

And suddenly he was there, his grin lighting up the dim little space to the side of the stage like a beacon shining in the dark, his misty blue eyes immediately seeking her out as though it was implicitly understood that she was the one who needed his assurance the most.

'You look terrific,' he told her.

Even as he spoke, Jake was thinking that she looked much better than that. *She looked nothing less than drop-dead gorgeous.* The purple velvet top she had selected on their shopping trip clung to her body in all the right places and her long black skirt skimmed the flat plane of her stomach and the soft swell of her hips as though it had been exclusively designed for her shape and her shape alone. Inevitably, his blood headed immediately south. Even if Caitlin couldn't sing a note, the men in the crowd were going to give her a lot of rope and that was a fact. It heartened him to know that they were all going to be pleasantly surprised.

'Trust me. You haven't got a thing to worry about. Just go out there and sing like you do in rehearsals, but even better.

If you get nervous, then just focus on me…I'll be out front as soon as you get onstage.'

'Okay. I'll do that… I can do that.' Caitlin managed to summon up a smile from only God knew where.

Eager to add his own brand of reassurance, Rick ran his hands up and down the sides of her slim arms and planted a sound kiss on her cheek. 'Just for luck, beautiful…not that you're going to need it.'

She barely opened her eyes during the first few bars of the opening number. It was much easier to simply shut out the sight of the crowd so that she could sing. She had been taken aback by the vociferous welcome they'd received from the fans when they walked onto the stage, somehow not expecting it to be quite as effusive as it had been. They didn't know her yet, and Caitlin had a lot to prove…

However, she was quickly swept away by the music and the need to sing, and as the wall of sound crashed over her she patted her thigh in time with the beat and started to enjoy herself. She was sure that performing in front of an audience must be an even bigger adrenaline rush than shooting rapids, and nothing had ever felt so right or so perfect.

That was when she finally opened her eyes. *That was when she saw Jake…*

He was clapping along with the rest of the crowd, watchful and silently assessing, his features so handsome and compelling that several women in the audience furtively glanced his way whether they were with someone or not. Releasing a long breath, Caitlin gave him a brief smile, then turned her attention back to the avid sea of faces in front of her.

Many people were capturing her and the band with their mobile phone cameras. She could almost feel the tangible sense of surprise in the air, the pleasure—and beneath the cool black satin of her long flowing skirt her legs couldn't help trembling. Steve Bridges gave her an extra drumroll to indicate his approval, and to her left Mike Casey muttered low, for her ears only, 'You're going to have them eating out of your hands, Cait.'

And she *did*. By the time they'd finished the final number of the night the crowd was with her all the way, cheering and clapping and stamping their feet for more. As baptisms of fire went, Caitlin couldn't have wished for a more favourable flame.

Backstage, she ran the gauntlet of well-wishers, road crew and fans alike, arriving in the small room the band had been allocated to more back-slapping, applause and champagne...courtesy of Jake. She barely registered the burst of bubbles on her tongue because everything felt so surreal. However, she *did* register the satisfying feel of Jake's strong arm wound possessively round her waist.

If anybody speculated on the 'extra-special' attention she was getting, no one dared voice it—least of all Rick, who was watching them with a stern 'headmaster' scowl as he bellowed to no one in particular that he needed another beer and *fast*.

Outside, as the venue emptied and the road crew loaded the van with Blue Sky's equipment—'Tank' and Dave, stalwarts of the industry, who had worked with Jake many times before—Rick pulled Caitlin aside as she was about to step up and get into Jake's familiar black car.

Jake had given her his keys and told her he wouldn't be long. He was still inside, checking arrangements for the following night when they would play their second and final London gig. There would be an even bigger crowd the next night, he'd told her, because the press would have got wind of her performance via the comments posted on social media sites and would come to check it out.

As Caitlin stood waiting to hear what Rick had to say, right on cue it started to rain.

'Is something the matter?' she asked warily.

'I don't know. You tell me.'

'Now you're being cryptic.' She started to smile, but straight away saw Rick wasn't in the mood to be placated.

'Is something going on between you and Jake?' he demanded.

Her stomach plummeted to her boots.

'And don't tell me you don't know what I mean.'

His hazel eyes were accusing and his shaggy blond hair was beginning to wave even more in the rain. Tugging up the collar of her raincoat, Caitlin shuddered.

It had been an amazing night. She had not only overcome her trepidation at singing in public, she had really begun to live her dream. She was bursting to talk to Lia and tell her all about it. Up until just a moment ago she'd wanted to shout out her news to the whole world. *I did it! I really am a singer in a bona fide rock band!* But now, as she gazed anxiously back at Rick, she felt as though someone had got a pin and deliberately popped her balloon.

'There's nothing going on between me and Jake other than him looking out for me and helping me settle in...with the band, I mean.'

'We can't afford another screw-up after the Marcie debacle. If you end up walking out on everyone because you got too involved with Jake then it will have serious implications for the band. I don't think they deserve that after all their hard work...do you?'

'No. Of course I don't.'

Caitlin knew what Rick was saying was only right, and she had no intention of letting anyone down. Just because Jake had put his arm round her when she'd come off stage and bought champagne to celebrate it didn't mean that the man was any more trustworthy than Sean. She had already intuited that f she had a physical relationship with him then her heart would seriously be at risk—because any woman with an ounce of common sense could easily see that he wasn't the type of man to commit to anything more meaningful. And Caitlin wasn't the type of woman to be intimate with a man and then forget it…as if were no more important than a trip to the hairdresser…

She lifted her chin. 'Don't worry, Rick. I promise you that the band comes first. Besides, I'm not looking to get personally involved with anyone.'

Liar. Nobody wanted to be alone for ever. And she wasn't the only girl in the world who hoped to find love again after the heartache of a failed relationship.

'Then we understand each other?' Rick reached out his hand to wipe away a raindrop glistening on her cheek.

'Understand what, exactly?' a deep male voice intoned.

CHAPTER EIGHT

Jake had walked up behind them. Straight away you could have cut the tension with a knife. Caitlin found herself wishing she hadn't agreed to stay the night at his flat. If it was going to make things this awkward between the two men, then she'd see if she could locate a cheap hotel for herself.

When neither she nor Rick rushed to answer his question, the glance he gave them was searing.

'I said, *understand what*, exactly? We'll stand here all night in the rain if we have to, until I get an answer.'

Rick hefted a sigh. 'Okay, Jake, if you really want to know then I'll tell you. I was warning Cait about getting personally involved with you. Just a few weeks ago Marcie walked out, leaving us high and dry. By great good fortune and the gods of rock and roll we found Caitlin. The last thing we need is to screw up the band's chances because she might get hurt by you and end up leaving the band.'

'I won't leave the band—I told you!'

Exasperated and embarrassed, Caitlin wanted to shake Rick. Did he really think she was so naïve that she'd risk the fantastic opportunity she'd been given to sing with the band in favour of a fleeting romance with Jake? As far as she was concerned she was in Blue Sky for the long haul, whatever happened.

Jake also looked exasperated. 'If there's anything personal between me and Caitlin then that's where it stays… between the *two* of us. We're both agreed that the welfare of the band comes first. I've been in this business long enough to know where my priorities lie. Now, it's been a long night, and Caitlin ought to get some rest if she's going to give another good performance tomorrow.'

'Under the circumstances, perhaps she'd better stay at my place instead?' His jaw clenched, Rick defied the taller man to give him an argument.

But Jake wasn't having any of it.

'I've given you my decision, and as far as I'm concerned it doesn't need debating.' With a ferocious scowl he grabbed the car keys out of Caitlin's hand and shouldered past her.

She stared at the other man. 'Why did you have to go and say that?'

'Because somebody has to look out for you, sweetheart. Jake is my best buddy, as well as my boss, but the truth is he doesn't have the best track record where women are concerned. Apart from with his ex—a relationship which probably scarred him for life—he doesn't go in for long relationships. I'm sure you know what I mean? And you're not like any of the other girls he's been with. You're sensitive, for a start. If you get too involved with him and he dumps you, you won't be able to take it on the chin and simply put it down to experience.'

'And what about you, Rick? Have *you* got a better track record? Anyway, contrary to opinion, I'm quite capable of taking care of myself. This is like a dream come true for me, to sing with this band, and I don't intend to mess it up, believe me.'

Behind them Jake started up the car's engine. Glancing round, Caitlin found his unsettling blue gaze blazing back at her through the windscreen.

She turned back to Rick. 'I've got to go.'

Saying no more, she walked to the car and got in without a word. She was still fumbling with her seatbelt when the vehicle pulled away from the kerb with a loud squeal of rubber on Tarmac.

* * *

Jake made a final check on Caitlin where she slept in his bedroom…*in his bed*…and then quietly closed the door behind him. In the large and airy living room, with the blinds pulled down and the blond oak floor cool beneath his feet, he dropped down onto a futon-style armchair. Then he leaned back to stare broodingly up at the ceiling.

Rick had no right, warning Caitlin not to get involved with him. What the hell did his friend think he was doing? Had Jake ever interfered in Rick's many and varied 'relationships'? No—he'd stood back and watched the fall out so many times it wasn't funny. *But then Rick wasn't contemplating having a hot, steamy affair with the band's gorgeous new singer, was he?*

Jake was only too aware that if he went ahead and had an affair with Caitlin it would be an extremely foolish and risky thing to do, with perhaps irreparable consequences. If he had any respect for the guys in the band—*and he had that in spades*—he shouldn't even be considering it. But then he hadn't achieved the success he had enjoyed by *not* taking risks. He wasn't setting out to break Caitlin's heart, but if they did get involved for a while he'd make it clear that he was only responding to an undeniable physical attraction that he couldn't resist.

If she felt the same then there wouldn't be a problem. If she *didn't* then Jake would simply have to put the whole thing down to experience and do his best to turn away from her in that department. Although God knew it wouldn't be easy.

Maybe once upon a time he'd nurtured a secret hope that he'd find a girl, settle down and eventually raise a family, but that hope hadn't survived for long. *Jodie had seen to that.* He didn't know if he would ever trust another woman again. *Having had a mother who had abandoned him was bad enough.* Discovering that his wife had been having an affair—and with someone who had such a high profile that the press would have a field-day—Jake hadn't had a prayer of protecting himself. Especially not when, in typically mercenary fashion, Jodie had concocted a vindictive story about their marriage and given the media carte blanche to say what the hell they liked about him. *He wasn't in a hurry to get burned a second time.*

Blowing out a breath, he let his jaded gaze take inventory of his surroundings. The fashionable and expensive apartment might be just a stone's throw from the King's Road in Chelsea, but its distinctly minimalist decor and general air of emptiness were testament to the fact that he was hardly ever there. Since leaving the children's home all those years ago he'd been regularly on the move—never staying in one place for any notable length of time.

Helplessly, he found his thoughts returning to Caitlin. If he was frank with her—made it clear that he was one of life's gypsies and wasn't looking for anything long-term or permanent—would she yield her body and a little of her time until the flames of desire they ignited together burned themselves out? And afterwards would they still be able to maintain a working relationship, see each other every day and have no regrets?

'You're a real prize, Jake Sorenson. You know that?'

Despising himself, because what he was prepared to offer her wasn't really very much at all, he pushed to his feet and paced the floor, restless and on edge because the woman he was crazy about was sleeping just a few feet away from him in the next room...in *his* bed...*alone.*

She had barely said a word to him when he'd brought her back to the flat. She had simply looked at him with those soulful green eyes of hers and made a polite comment that the flat was 'really beautiful', then walked round the living room examining every single print that decorated the walls as if fascinated.

They were mostly artistic photographic prints of well-known music artists Jake had worked with, along with one or two high-profile fashion models who had worked on video shoots. As Caitlin had studied them it had become eminently clear to him that not one of them could hold a candle to her.

He should have told her how beautiful she'd looked tonight, how great she'd done, that she'd made them all proud. But he had been too keyed up because he'd been fighting to keep the lid on his attraction. And Rick's warning had kept going round and round in his head like a mantra that was hard to shut out. So they'd had a cup of coffee, some brief conversation about nothing very much, and then he'd shown her into the bedroom.

It hadn't just been him and the band who had loved her performance tonight. The audience had loved her too. But, drawing on his extensive experience, Jake knew it wasn't all going to be plain sailing. Audiences were notoriously fickle until they really got to know a band, and they'd encounter all sorts on this tour before it was finished. *There would be criticisms, too.* Jake just hoped that Caitlin could handle them.

But there was no doubt in his mind that, with her talent and beauty, Blue Sky could win themselves a prestigious recording contract. As long as they were consistently able to come up with the goods he had the contacts and the know-how to help make all their dreams come true. *Except maybe his own...*

Once again his thoughts turned to the beautiful girl asleep in his bed. She was a dark-haired enchantress, with a face and a body that could enslave *any* man, and Jake had undoubtedly fallen under her spell. Cursing beneath his breath, he headed determinedly towards the bathroom and a long, cold, hopefully passion-killing shower.

The distinct sound of music playing disturbed him. For a few moments Jake just lay still, staring up at the ceiling. He was lying on the rarely used spare bed in the flat's guest room, but he'd phoned ahead to the caretaking agency he used for someone to come in and tidy the place and make up the beds with fresh sheets before they arrived.

Blinking away his disorientation as he properly came to, he realised that the radio was playing in the kitchen. *Caitlin*. She must be up and about. At the thought of the woman who had given him yet another sleepless night he groaned and propped himself up on his elbow. Then he dragged the fingers of his free hand through his tousled dark hair.

Glancing down at the distinctive bulge beneath the sheet, Jake released a long, slow breath. Jumping out of bed straight away wasn't an option when he was so heavily and obviously aroused. Better that he wait for a few minutes and concentrate his thoughts on something either mundane or unpleasant to help dispel the heat in his groin. But that was no easy task, with Caitlin beginning to join in the chorus of the song on the radio, her sexy tones making him tingle all over just as if she were lying next to him, crooning softly into his ear.

A few moments later she was knocking at his door. 'Jake, are you up yet? I've made you a cup of tea.'

Caitlin sounded so damn cheerful that he wanted to get up, drag her inside, throw her down on the bed and have his wicked way with her without further ado.

He released another heartfelt groan.

'That word doesn't get mentioned round here in the morning. I'm strictly a coffee man,' he grumbled, plumping up his pillow and jamming it behind his back.

'No problem. I can just as easily make you some coffee. How do you like it?'

'Hot, dark and sultry, with a little bit of sugar…just like my women.'

'I see you've recovered your sense of humour…'

'Apparently I have.'

Jake couldn't believe he was having this conversation through a closed door. He glared at the offending wood panel as if his gaze had the power to burn a hole through it.

From the other side Caitlin remarked brightly, 'By the way, thanks for giving up your bed to me. I hope you were comfortable too. Did you sleep all right?'

What a question!

He rubbed a hand round his beard-roughened jaw. Rocks on the desert floor couldn't have been more uncomfortable. He'd tossed and turned so much that he felt every single day of his thirty-six years this morning. *And little Miss Hole-in-her-Stocking wasn't helping, with her cheery wide-awake tone that conveyed she'd slept like a baby...*

'No, I didn't,' he growled.

There was no response.

For a few moments Jake thought his guest had returned to the kitchen. Then, to his surprise, the door opened and she walked into the bedroom. Wearing tight faded jeans, and a loose-fitting white T-shirt with clearly no bra underneath it, Caitlin fixed him with a tentative gaze. A soft flush suffused her cheeks when the corners of his mouth crooked upwards in a smile.

'Something wrong?' he asked huskily.

'You said that you didn't sleep?'

The way she said it let him know she was concerned, guilty, or both. It was too good an opportunity to waste and Jake wasn't a man who ever let a good opportunity sail by without grabbing onto it.

'Yeah...I might just stay put for a while longer and catch up a little.'

Caitlin couldn't take her eyes off Jake's heavenly chest. He was all lean, rippling muscle, rock-hard stomach and tanned flesh. With his sexy tousled hair and sleepy-eyed expression, the man was as handsome and seductive as a mythical warrior. And what did she think she was doing, daring to come into his room and stare at him as if she'd come to pay homage to one of the gods?

It was perhaps inevitable that he should pat the space

next to him in the luxurious bed and suggest, 'Why don't you come and join me?'

'I slept well. I don't need any more rest.'

'Did I mention rest?'

Caitlin swallowed hard. 'No, but…it doesn't look like there's a lot of room,' she said nervously.

Suddenly she was so aroused that it was impossible to pretend indifference. Jake was one sexy, charismatic specimen and she was only human. Could she help it if her neglected libido was nearing boiling point and needing resolution? Heat was already seeping up her thighs, between her legs, making her moist, while the sensitive tips of her nipples tingled painfully against her shirt.

'You underneath, me on top…how much room do we need?' Jake parried seductively, his blue eyes drowsy with desire. 'We can make it work.'

It was an outrageous suggestion and Caitlin didn't dare take him up on it…*did she?*

Glancing up at the faint morning light filtering through the slats of the rolled-down blinds, she was suddenly consumed by an avalanche of doubt. And not just doubt at her ability to get herself out of trouble when the situation demanded it, but at putting her common sense versus a desire so red-hot it was already burning her.

The sheer, unmitigated sensual tug of Jake sitting up in bed, with his chest bared and his eyes goading her towards something so deliciously sinful that it made her weak just thinking about it, was in the end too hard to resist.

With her heart thudding, she replied, 'I've never…I've never gone in for casual sex. I just wanted you to know that. Do you have some protection?'

He stared. 'I've got everything we need right here.'

Jake had known he'd finally lost his battle against temptation as soon as Caitlin had walked into the room. The longing to hold her in his arms and to know her intimately had finally overridden all sense of right and wrong.

He wasn't aiming to hurt either her or the band. He had too much respect for all of them for that. He was merely following an irresistible impulse that wouldn't be denied. That said, there would be nothing casual about sex between him and Caitlin. Even though she was gorgeous—the ultimate male fantasy come to life—Jake admired her for the courageous woman she was.

He sighed with pleasure. Beneath the thin protection of her virginal white shirt her aroused nipples were practically drilling a hole thought the material, and he knew that if he touched her at the apex between her delectable thighs she would be hot and ready for him straight away. The thought slowed and thickened the blood coursing through his veins. It was like being drip-fed with unadulterated honey. And he was so desperate for her, so hungry, that if she didn't soon join him he seriously thought he might explode.

Her hands were shaking as Caitlin undid the zipper on her jeans and stepped out of them. Then she nervously moved towards the edge of the bed, dressed in nothing but the T-shirt and white cotton panties. The scalding, hungry gaze that Jake pinned her with was so blatantly carnal she thought she would melt. No man had ever looked at her with such unfettered desire in his eyes before, with such wild, primitive heat.

Low-voiced, he murmured, 'Why don't you take off your shirt'

What's a girl to do? Caitlin thought wildly. Then simply did as he asked.

A carnal whirlpool had rolled over her, snatching her up in its maelstrom so completely that there was nothing she could do but give up struggling and let it carry her where it would.

Her movements were unknowingly sensual and provocative as she pulled her shirt over her head to remove it. Her full, perfectly rounded breasts with their dusky dark nipples jutted towards him and every delectable line and curve of her sexy body was revealed in all its glory. Her small, slender waist, the voluptuous swell of her hips and her smooth, shapely thighs all came under his hungry scrutiny as he gazed his fill.

When she finally removed the shirt and let it fall to the floor her flowing dark hair drifted silkily across her breasts and partially hid them from view.

'Shall I take these off too?' she asked shyly, indicating the white panties.

'No.' Jake reached towards her and pulled her firmly down onto the bed. 'That particular pleasure is going to be mine.'

With her hair spilling wildly across her face, Caitlin gulped down a shocked breath as he slid expert hands down over her hips and practically ripped off the flimsy underwear.

'Jake, I—' But whatever she'd intended saying next was cut off by the hot press of his mouth and the skilful invasion of his tongue seeking hers as his heavily aroused manhood pressed deeply into her soft belly.

Her senses were all but overwhelmed by his intoxicating heat and the erotic masculine scents of his body. One of his hands slid across her breast, rubbing and kneading the already inflamed nipple, nipping and squeezing until she gasped her pleasure into his mouth and bucked her hips against his. *It was clear they were singing from the same song-sheet.* His mouth closing over her nipple, Jake suckled hard and Caitlin whimpered her delight.

Lifting his head, he breathed, 'I've got to take care of something...'

Reaching across to a nearby chair, where he'd left his jeans, he delved into a pocket and withdrew a foil packet. He wasted no time in expertly tearing it open. Sheathed in the protection, Jake turned his attention back to Caitlin, kneeing her slim thighs apart to insert an explorative finger into her moist heat.

Even as she gasped, she knew she was more than ready for him, and was gratified when he positioned his sex and thrust assuredly inside her. Her thoughts utterly deserted her as she drowned in an ecstatic pleasure like no other she'd ever experienced. The sheer emotion she felt at the wonder of it caused her eyes to fill with tears. Then she cried out as Jake's mouth found the hollow between her neck and shoulder and bit her there.

His lips sought hers again and his kiss was deep and hard as he thrust into her mouth with his tongue even as his sex filled her and he felt her scalding satin heat engulf him. If he died right now he'd die happy. He'd never experienced pleasure or desire like it. Beneath him, Caitlin writhed and moaned, her breath released in hot little gasps that seared his skin, and when she raised her hips to welcome him even more deeply, and suddenly convulsed round him, she cried out for a second time and he saw that her beautiful emerald eyes were moist with tears. Her expression was stunned. She looked like a woman who had never experienced the full orgasmic impact of climax before.

The mere thought undid Jake. Within seconds he was thrusting even deeper, whispering against her ear how beautiful she was, how perfect. Then his own desire and need reached its crescendo and he was swept away on a cascade of a joy so fierce and so perfect that he had no words to describe it. In fact it stunned him to silence.

His blue eyes glittering with feeling, he manoeuvred himself carefully to lie down beside her and with his fingers gently traced the exquisite line of her jaw. 'Caitlin?'

'What?'

Jake was stroking her ear, securing a silken strand of long ebony hair behind it. Gazing back into the incandescent eyes that looked like bewitching green fire, he silently acknowledged that he'd never experienced such depth and strength of emotion lying with a woman before. He only knew that he had the sense of feeling strangely privileged.

'I think you're the most beautiful woman I've ever known.'

Even as his words lifted her spirits higher than they'd ever been lifted before, Caitlin was already missing the warm heavy press of his body. She wanted to tell him to come back, to love her again and never stop... Only the icy fronds of harsh reality swept through her like winter just then.

She thought, *But he doesn't love me, does he? All we enjoyed together just now was great sex.*

The fact that she'd never even got close to orgasm with Sean, and that more often than not she'd seen to her own needs after the event, would hardly register with Jake. Besides, a properly committed relationship wasn't what he was looking for, was it? They both knew that. When he stopped desiring her body Caitlin would just have to learn to concentrate all her energies on her singing and view him solely as Blue Sky's manager.

Could she do that? Could she cut off her emotions so easily when what had just taken place between her and Jake had been nothing less than earth-shattering? *Her whole world had been utterly changed forever.* Did he realise that just the merest touch from him was enough to set her on fire, to make her need him as much as she needed to breathe?

Glancing back into his steady blue gaze, she wondered how it was possible for a man to have such luxuriant long lashes and still be so incredibly masculine. Perhaps it was the hard, lean jaw, with that slight indentation in the chin, or was it the exquisitely shaped mouth with the slightly fuller lower lip? A mouth made for passion...for the erotic pleasures only shared by lovers.

Of course it went without saying that Jake must have had a few of those...perhaps more than Caitlin cared to know about. Right now the thought of even *one* was enough to make her heart jolt sickeningly.

'That's high praise, coming from a man like you,' she

answered, affecting a light, breezy tone to shield her true feelings from him.

He frowned. 'What do you mean, a man like me?'

'I just mean you must have known many beautiful women. I won't kid myself that I'm particularly special.'

Now his handsome visage looked perturbed. 'Hey. Why say that? Don't you know how much pleasure you've just given me? You mesmerise and intoxicate me, Caitlin. Sharing what we just shared was beyond wonderful.'

Caitlin couldn't help but smile—even as she came to a distressing conclusion about what she had to do for *both* their sakes.

'Thank you. I'm glad you think that. I thought so too. But now I think we should both come back down to earth, don't you?'

Lightly removing Jake's hand from where it lay across her stomach, she rolled over and leant down to pick up the clothes she'd discarded on the floor.

'Where do you think you're going?'

He sounded surprised, upset. Not immediately answering, Caitlin stepped into her panties, then got to her feet. She hurriedly pulled on her T-shirt and quickly got into her jeans, sensing him watching her broodingly.

'Are you going to tell me what's going on? Why the sudden urgency to get up when we can take our time? We can stay here all day if we want. There's no hurry.'

Combing back her hair with trembling fingers, she turned to face him.

'I suddenly came to my senses, that's all. Hopefully, now that we've got this out of our system, we can get back to normal and concentrate on work. I think we should both ensure that what happened between us won't happen again, Jake. From now on our relationship should be strictly about the band. Now that I'm clear about our priorities I'll go and get a quick shower and then make some coffee.' She started to move towards the door.

'Forget the damn coffee, woman!' Jake threw back the covers on the bed, to all intents and purposes coming after her. 'Come back here and get into bed.'

'Why?' Despite her resolution not to let herself down by crying, Caitlin knew her eyes were already filling with tears. 'So that I can be even more reckless and stupid than I've been already?'

When he didn't answer but instead shook his head, as if her outburst was totally incomprehensible, she flew out through the door without another word and headed determinedly for the bathroom.

CHAPTER NINE

I'M SORRY I didn't talk to you a bit more about how I felt. Silently rehearsing the words, Caitlin wished she'd said them out loud to Jake before he'd abruptly left the flat that morning to go God only knew where.

He'd barely acknowledged her when he got up, and when he'd emerged from the bathroom he'd simply told her he was going out for a while and slammed the door. His cold manner had made her want to curl up into a little ball and disappear. Even as he'd moved towards the door Caitlin had wanted to plead with him to stay.

It was evident that she'd soured things by getting out of bed and declaring that they should come back down to earth and concentrate on the band. Even though it was the sensible thing to do, the *right* thing, she knew it wouldn't make either of them happy. How could it, when the intensity of their lovemaking had clearly demonstrated how strong their attraction was? Would doing the right thing help them to deny it?

Weary with going over the same ground over and over again without resolution, she diverted her restless energy with undertaking a little light cleaning round the flat. Although it was obvious that the fashionably minimalist living quarters barely needed it, to Caitlin's mind it was better to do *something* rather than sit there twiddling her thumbs and worrying herself sick about what had happened.

She would never regret their lovemaking. How could she ever regret revelling in the joy of being a woman, in the power of her body to give and receive such mind-blowing pleasure as she had done with Jake? Their brief union had stirred feelings and emotions long buried, and she couldn't be angry about that. Not when her body still glowed and throbbed with the attention he'd given her.

And even if he hadn't been motivated by love, the truth was…Caitlin *had*. There was no longer any point in denying it.

Locating a vacuum cleaner and duster, she cleaned the flat to within an inch of its life. When all the surfaces gleamed to her satisfaction, and the living room sang with the scent of beeswax, she opened the windows to allow fresh air to circulate. Then she went into the kitchen to make herself some toast and coffee.

Her appetite taken care of, she retreated to the living room to browse a lone copy of a glossy music magazine. Her attention was immediately caught by an interesting little snippet ringed in red. It was all about Jake.

What's former music promoter and artist supremo Jake Sorenson up to these days? Rumour has it he's gone back to his roots and is managing a tight little foursome called Blue Sky. After the lead songstress Marcie Wallace recently walked out, a little bird told yours truly that the search is on for a dazzling new diva to replace her.

All we know is that she'll have to be pretty exceptional to meet Jake's well-known exacting standards. Remember that this is the man who made his fortune bringing world-class bands Soft Rain and The Butterfly Net to prominence, then dropped out into self-imposed obscurity for five years after a vindictive exposé by his ex, Jodie Parks.

Knowing Mr Sorenson's famed proclivity for discovering matchless talent, we'd seriously advise watching this space…

'"Dazzling diva"? Are they serious?'

Chewing anxiously on the inside of her cheek, Caitlin dropped the magazine onto the small mahogany table as though she'd suddenly been burnt. Because the idea of her being a diva in any shape or form was preposterous.

She leant back into the cream-coloured futon and gathered a cushion close to try and absorb the shock and disbelief that rolled through her. Yes, she'd made a good start with the band—she'd dipped her toe in the water and got her feet wet, and the enthusiastic reception from the audience last night had been more, *much* more than she'd hoped for. But could she come up with the goods night after night for the next three weeks without letting herself and the others down?

Her fingers tentatively stroked down the sensitive skin of her throat. She'd have to seriously think about taking better care of her voice, for one thing. That aside, her most pressing thought right now was Jake. Where on earth had he got to? Was he still mad at her for deserting him so abruptly this morning?

It stunned her to realise that she was in love with him. She hadn't been in the market for a relationship and hadn't intended to be for a very long time. But then she'd never dreamed fate would bring a man like Jake into her life. A man who one minute wanted her as much as he wanted to take his next breath and the next...

Her insides knotted anxiously, and because the feeling so unsettled her she jumped up and went in search of some window cleaner and a cloth and started to clean the windows.

'What the hell do you think you're doing?'

Caitlin nearly fell off the chair she was precariously balanced on. Even with its aid, the glass corners of the window frame were particularly tricky to get to. But it was hard to believe she'd been so absorbed that she'd somehow blotted out the sound of Jake's key in the door and had therefore been unprepared for his appearance.

She turned to observe him. 'What does it look like I'm doing?'

'You'd better get down from there before you break your neck!'

Before she could react Jake had moved across to her and caught her by the waist. Then he unceremoniously hoisted her off the chair. Caitlin felt her face flame red.

'Stop treating me like a child, will you? I'm perfectly capable of cleaning a few windows without supervision.'

'That might be the case, but who in hell asked you to clean the windows in the first place? I hire someone from a cleaning firm to do that. I hired *you* to sing in a band, not become my domestic.'

Jake glanced impatiently around him and Caitlin saw him register the spotless parquet floor, the plumped-up cushions on his easy chairs and futon, the shining glass on his framed prints. Aware that his hands still lingered at the sides of her waist, she wished her heart wouldn't beat quite so fast—because his touch was already making her feel weak.

'I can't help it' She shrugged, 'I always clean when I get tense. I can't stand inactivity...not having something to do.' Her teeth clamped down on her lip.

'I see.'

Beneath his impenetrable glare, she felt like a small child being told off by her parent.

Because she was nervous, she remarked thoughtlessly, 'By the way, I notice that you don't have many personal photos around?'

As soon as the words were out Caitlin wanted the floor to open up and swallow her.

Jake's expression was immediately dismayed. 'If by "personal photos" you mean of family, then you know very well that I don't have any.'

Her insides turned over. 'I...I'm so sorry I said that. I was just nervous. But personal photos could equally mean friends. Didn't you have any close pals when you were young?'

When he didn't immediately comment, she felt as if the hole she'd just dug herself had got even deeper.

'You mean at the children's home? Not really.'

His tone was chillingly matter-of-fact. Caitlin knew she should steer the conversation away from his heartbreaking childhood as quickly as possible, but care and concern for him made her not want to shy away from it.

'Do you mind if I ask how you came to grow up in a children's home, Jake?'

'My mother gave me up because she was just sixteen when she fell pregnant with me and in her wisdom decided to have me adopted. Only I *wasn't* adopted. I was hard to place because I was born with a heart murmur. The people at the children's home told me that most interested adoptive parents were wary of taking on a sick baby.' Shrugging, he shaped his lips into a sardonic smile. 'Not that I minded... it was their loss. As I grew older I realised what an asset it was to be left alone by people. I learned to enjoy my own company, to pursue my own interests without interference.'

Caitlin stared, trying hard to assimilate everything she'd heard. 'And what about the heart murmur? Do you still see a doctor or specialist?'

'No. I grew out of it. It got better all by itself. It hasn't been an issue since I was young. Anyway, are you going to tell me what's making you so tense, or do I have to guess?'

Suddenly impatient, he relieved her of the scrunched-up cleaning rag she was still holding onto and threw it onto the window ledge.

As Caitlin fought hard to marshal her thoughts, Jake sucked in a breath and let it out again slowly. 'I don't want you to worry about what happened between us.'

'I'm not. I mean, I was just...I was just...'

He held up his hand to indicate she should stop talking. His blue eyes glittered. 'Hear me out. I don't want you to worry about it because I don't regret a damn thing. And, contrary to what you might think, I'm not going to pretend it never happened.'

A warm rush climbed into her chest. The anxiety that had propelled her into her frenetic cleaning bout slowly subsided, leaving her with a sense of joy so acute she couldn't resist the smile that tugged at her lips.

He didn't regret it… That surely had to signify something, didn't it?

'However,' he continued, 'even though I won't pretend it never happened, I agree we can't risk a repeat performance. You were right when you said we should concentrate on the band.'

Caitlin's brief joy was quickly replaced by crushing disappointment. It was so intense that it was as though all the breath had been brutally sucked from her lungs.

'You think that's the best idea?' she murmured.

'It's not because I don't want us to be together again like we were this morning…'

Capturing her wrist, Jake firmly wove his fingers through her own. His misty blue eyes mesmerised her, and she saw that he was hungry for her again—and yet it was clear he was furious with himself. She suddenly realised that he didn't *want* to desire her so much, and was furious because she was hardly helping him to resist.

'You got into this because you wanted to realise a dream,' he went on. 'One day soon this band is going to be very successful…that is if we're all committed to the same goal. If you and I don't maintain a professional relationship then the whole thing could fall apart. I think that would be a great shame, don't you?'

She wasn't going to disagree. With a brief nod she dropped her gaze. To her surprise, Jake released her hand, slid his fingers beneath her jaw and lifted her chin.

'I've been to see Rick and I've arranged to stay over at his place tonight. You can stay here. Treat the place as if it was your own. I'll be over to pick you up at about six. We'll do a sound-check and run through the playlist. Tomorrow, when we go to Brighton, I've booked you into a separate hotel from the rest of us—a much nicer hotel, because you deserve a little luxury. All in all, I think the arrangement is for the best.'

Caitlin swallowed hard.

'Why? Don't you trust me, Jake? I'd much rather be in the same hotel as everyone else. Do you think that because we made love I'm going to make a nuisance of myself?'

Hurt cramping her throat, she pulled out of his grasp and strode across to the other side of the room. Folding her arms, she stared blankly up at a large photographic print of a beautiful redhead. The sight of it made her even sadder when she remembered that there weren't any more personal photos around because Jake had no family. It broke her heart to think that he'd grown up without someone to love him.

'Are you crazy?' he ground out. 'It's *me* I don't trust. It's like I told you before—I have a job to do and a little bit of distance wouldn't be a bad thing right now…at least when we're not working together.'

Everything he said made the utmost sense, but it didn't prevent Caitlin from feeling desperately disappointed. Hope was futile, she realised. She didn't have a right to hope for anything as far as Jake Sorenson was concerned. And thank goodness at least one of them was taking charge of the situation. Of *course* it was right that the band should come first.

Wasn't her passion for music and singing the reason she had auditioned in the first place? It certainly hadn't been because she was looking for another relationship. And she was sure she wasn't looking for some 'on-off' hot little liaison with Blue Sky's charismatic manager. The sooner she let Jake see that she wasn't going to waste her time crying over spilt milk, the better.

'It sounds like you've taken care of everything. Good. I

can't say I'm not glad about that. Rick was right when he said it would a bad idea, making things personal between us.'

'Leave Rick out of this' with a grim scowl Jake walked angrily towards her. 'What's between you and me is no-body's business but our own. You got that?'

What could Caitlin do beneath that frosty glare but acquiesce? Even if what he had just said contradicted everything he'd said previously. Their relationship *wasn't* just their own business—wasn't that the point? Blue Sky had a vested interest in her not having a personal relationship with their manager. They were probably concerned that Jake would break her heart and she would end up leaving the band…just as Marcie had.

Perhaps it really *was* for the best if Caitlin and Jake pretended that their passionate liaison hadn't happened after all. If Jake could be cool about it then she would just have to learn to do the same.

That night, having heard positive feedback about Blue Sky's performance the previous night, the music press turned out in force. Onstage, determinedly giving her all, Caitlin had had to contend with flashbulbs popping in her face at regular intervals and backstage afterwards it was even worse.

A huge number of people had squeezed into a room not much bigger than a cloakroom. The atmosphere was hot, stuffy and claustrophobic, and the smell of alcohol mingled liberally with the accumulated heat of bodies pressing in too close. All she really wanted to do was to get back to Jake's flat and escape.

The sense of panic that gripped her had taken her by surprise, and she'd more or less clammed up when too many questions had been catapulted her way by over-zealous reporters who barely gave her even a second to answer them. If it hadn't been for Jake, dealing with their questions with cool professionalism, as well as Rick protecting her from the crush, Caitlin would have fled in a heartbeat—never mind that publicity *any* publicity…was meant to be good.

Mid-morning the next day found her sitting in the foyer of the old-fashioned seafront hotel in Brighton that Jake had booked the band into, delicately hiding a yawn behind her hand as Rick and Jake conversed with the desk clerk. The rest of the band members were out on the small square patio, chatting. Caitlin stifled another guilty yawn as she watched them.

'Are we keeping you awake, Cait?'

Taking her by surprise, Rick gave her shoulder an affectionate squeeze, then dropped down beside her on the padded seat, stirring the air around them with the musky scent of his cologne.

'I couldn't sleep last night.' Shrugging her shoulders in the faded denim jacket she wore over a blue maxi-dress, she attempted a smile.

'Excitement keeping you up, huh?'

Rick was grinning, and she saw her companion's astute hazel eyes were curious. 'Something like that,' Caitlin replied.

Let him think that, she decided. It was a lot less complicated than confessing that she'd been missing Jake. That her body had been aching for him all night.

She would swear that she'd tossed and turned from midnight to dawn because she needed him so much. No wonder she felt as if she could sleep for England this morning!

Jake had bunked down over at Rick's, and the Chelsea flat had been soulless and empty without him. Even last night's undoubted success and the ensuing interest from the press hadn't been able to console her.

Was it really so wrong that she should want Jake as badly as she did? Her gaze helplessly gravitated towards him as he leant casually back against the reception desk, his glance sweeping thoughtfully over her and Rick. Today, his long legs were encased in faded black denim, a leather belt with a buckle was slung low on his tight, lean hips and his leather jacket was folded casually across one arm. His expression made her heart turn over. She wondered if he'd had similar trouble getting to sleep last night.

As his searching glance deliberately sought hers Caitlin sensed the hot sizzle from the contact erupt in her belly like a flare.

'We've got a few things lined up for today, but perhaps you can catch up on some rest later on, before the gig tonight.'

With her face warmly glowing, Caitlin guiltily turned her attention back to Rick.

'Sounds good to me…what things?'

'You mean you don't know?'

'No, I don't.'

'Didn't Jake tell you about the photographs?'

'What photographs?'

'We're booked into a studio in a couple of hours.'

Jake was suddenly there in front of them.

'We're getting some promotional shots of the band.'

Caitlin refrained from commenting. She was wondering if a couple of hours would be enough to transform her sleepy-eyed expression into something half resembling awake. Aside from that, she *hated* having her photograph taken. Next to eating beetroot, it was right up there on the list of things that made her squirm.

'So be sure to wear something sexy,' Rick piped up with a grin. 'You're bound to give the current babes in the charts a run for their money!'

Caitlin immediately rounded on him with an affronted glare. 'The campaign for equal rights for women clearly just passed you by, didn't it? Why strive for intelligent observation when you can just go for the lowest common denominator?'

In his usual incorrigible fashion he returned, 'Because life is complicated enough, without trying to be clever. I'm a simple guy. Can I help it if I have an eye for beauty?'

'You've made your point, Rick.' Jake's blue eyes were icy as he flashed him a warning glare. 'Now, why don't you just leave it there?'

'Can I check into my hotel now?' Caitlin interjected quickly. 'If these photos are strictly necessary then I'd like to get a shower and make myself presentable before we go.'

Rising abruptly to her feet, she pulled the edges of her denim jacket more closely across her dress's scooped neckline. All the testosterone flying around was making her nervous.

'Sure—I'll take you. Let's go back to the car.' Jake handed Rick a bunch of key cards. 'You guys go and sort yourselves out. I'll make sure Caitlin is okay and catch up with you in about half an hour.'

Getting to his feet, Rick frowned. 'Gee, I wish taking care of our "best asset" was part of *my* job description. It can hardly seem like work, can it?' he quipped.

Almost imperceptibly Jake's shoulders stiffened. Feigning indifference to the undoubted tension between the two men, Caitlin started to walk away. But Jake caught hold of her elbow and led them across the shiny parquet floor towards the exit.

She shook off his hold. 'I'm quite capable of—'

'Not now, Caitlin.'

Without even sparing her a glance, he conveyed the fact that his temper was on a very short fuse. Only a fool would seek to ignite it, so she swallowed down her indignation and turned her attention to keeping pace with his long-legged stride.

Flipping off the top of a bottle of beer from the mini-bar in his room, Jake imbibed a generous draught of the ice-cold contents and then dropped back down onto the bed. Sounds of the city permeated the forest-green curtains he'd drawn to shut out the night, and inside the images on the television screen silently flickered.

He'd deliberately muted the sound, but for a moment or two his attention was caught by the intense expressions of two lovers bidding each other goodbye at a railway station. The corners of his mouth lifted in a smile and a warm feeling climbed steadily into his chest—but it wasn't just because of the touching scene. *The sight of the lovers had inevitably made him think of Caitlin.*

Her name alone had the power to convey feelings inside him that he scarcely knew what to do with. Watching her pose with the rest of the band that afternoon for photographs had been both heaven and hell. She'd worn fitted black jeans with a virginal white stretch top that had clung lovingly to her breasts, and at the photographer's behest had taken off her boots and socks to leave her feet sexily bare. With her river of ebony hair, sparkling green eyes and naturally beautiful smile, Jake's hadn't been the only jaw to hit the floor when she'd stood as instructed with the other band members to pose for the camera.

'Anyone need some ice to help them cool down?' Rick had quipped as they'd stood together, observing the proceedings, and the comment had made Jake feel far from friendly as he thought of his colleague fantasising about the woman who had so recently become his lover...the woman he was trying desperately hard not to want because protocol demanded he abstain.

Dismayed by the violence of his feelings, he'd taken a couple of steps back to compose himself as he'd wrestled with a near overwhelming urge to kidnap Caitlin after the shoot and take her back to his hotel room. That was when his imagination had gone into overdrive.

Groaning, he took another swig of beer and glared at the television as the thought of yet another cold shower made him want to grab the offending equipment and throw it out the window. *That would be a coup for the press...*the band manager at the centre of a scandal with his model ex-wife a few years ago drawing attention once again with a demonstration of typically 'rock star' behaviour in a hotel room.

Irritably dismissing the thought, Jake brought his attention back to Caitlin. She had yet again done them proud that night, her sexy, heaven-sent voice alternately whipping up the crowd or innocently seducing them, her vocals melding perfectly with the band's tight, rich sound. In just three short weeks she'd learned more, given more, and was shaping up into more of a professional than some people in the business he'd known for years. He might be biased, but Jake knew they were onto something good.

But if he didn't touch her again soon he would lose his mind. That was if he hadn't lost it already.

He stretched out his hand for the telephone next to the bed. He could at least talk to her, tell her... Tell her *what*, exactly? That he was going crazy just thinking about her? That he was desperate to hold her and demonstrate in no uncertain terms just how much he desired her?

He let the receiver clatter noisily back onto its rest. He couldn't do it. He wouldn't put Caitlin in such an untenable position. He'd just have to find some other way of working off all his nervous energy. *Was that the correct term for a raging libido these days?*

With a humourless smile, he drained the bottle of beer dry, then stood up and threw it into a nearby wastepaper bin. Then he reached for his jacket and slammed out through the door without even pausing to switch off the TV.

The jarring sound of a bell ringing right next to her ear had Caitlin burying her face into her lilac-coloured pillow in a bid to shut the noise out. *It must be someone's car alarm going off down the street—or a fire drill, perhaps.* Her mind played games with the sound, encouraging her to carry on sleeping. Someone would see to it soon, she thought vaguely.

Only all of a sudden she was wide awake and scrambling to sit up as it finally registered that it was the phone beside her bed that was ringing. Clamping the receiver to her ear, she impatiently pushed her hair away from her face and squinted at the glowing green digits blinking back at her from the alarm clock…

Two-thirty a.m.? What the…?

'Hello?'

'Caitlin. Were you asleep?'

Jake. At the sound of that gravelly bass voice her heartbeat accelerated like a rabbit being chased by a fox.

'What's the matter? Is anything wrong?'

Had something happened to him? Was he hurt? In trouble? Caitlin's fertile imagination went into overdrive.

'Nothing's wrong. I'm downstairs in the lobby. Can you come down?'

'It's half past two in the morning!'

'I'm quite aware of the time.'

God, it was so good to hear his voice.

'Why? I mean, why do you want me to come downstairs at this time of night?' Even as she asked the question she was swinging her legs out of bed and seeking out the jeans and warm red sweater she'd folded onto a chair.

'Because I want to see you.'

His tone immediately conveyed his impatience, making his statement sound more like an order than a request.

Caitlin frowned, 'You could see me in the morning after breakfast. I don't make much sense until I've had my cup of tea.'

'Damn it, Caitlin! Just put some clothes on and get down here, will you?'

Jake hung up on her, leaving her staring at the telephone as though it had suddenly sprouted a beak and a couple of wings.

Shaking herself out of the daze she was in, she hurried into the bathroom. Splashing her face with some cold water, she quickly brushed her teeth, then combed her dishevelled hair with her fingers. There was no time to even think about applying some make-up. At any rate, what did he expect? It was two-thirty in the morning, she was tired and dazed—and...if she admitted it...more hopeful than she had a right to be considering he'd kept her at a deliberate distance for the past two days.

Crossing her arms over her soft woollen sweater, she stepped warily out of the lift to find him waiting by the doors, his lean jaw dark with night-time shadow, his hair mussed and his piercing blue eyes preternaturally bright. Desire for him was like a flash flood, fierce and elemental, and it rendered her immediately weak.

'Jake...' His name on her lips was little more than a murmur.

'Come for a walk' he said, catching hold of her hand and urging her towards the rotating glass doors of the exit.

Mid-stride, Caitlin ground to a halt to stare at him. 'You want to go for a walk? Are you crazy? It's two-thirty in the morning.'

A muscle tensed visibly in his jaw and Caitlin allowed him to guide her outside. The wind cut through her like an icy blade and, catching her shiver, Jake immediately shrugged off his jacket and draped it around her shoulders.

Her eyes wide, she glanced up at him. 'What's all this about, Jake?'

'Come on—let's walk. It's too cold to stand around.'

They headed out towards the pier, Jake catching hold of her hand again as if it was the most natural thing in the world for him to do. The night sky was almost black, but there was still plenty of light. Aside from the stars and the curved sliver of moon that permeated the velvet blanket there was plenty of neon to light up the streets, and even the occasional car's headlamp as it flew past.

For most of the way Jake had stayed silent. Now he stopped, drawing Caitlin close against him before staring out to sea.

'You were amazing tonight.'

He turned back to survey her. Heat slid down her spine and radiated down into her pelvis. The unexpected compliment took her by surprise.

'Thanks...I really enjoyed myself. The band were great, weren't they? I particularly liked—'

Jake silenced her with a hard, hot kiss that made her stumble against him.

Her lips were like soft satin pillows that couldn't help but invite him to keep tasting them. But he didn't just want to kiss her. He wanted to do so much more... The very idea made him tighten. Then it made him hard.

Lifting his head, he examined the dazed expression she wore—the moist, softly opened mouth that he'd so spontaneously and heatedly ravished, and the shining green eyes that he defied any man not to lose his soul to.

'I'll go crazy if I can't make love to you soon,' he confessed.

'We can't. Remember, we agreed...?'

Emitting a curse, Jake stared at Caitlin and drove his hands through his already windblown hair in frustration.

'I know what we agreed. I know what we *should* do. But the truth is that when you were posing with the others today at the photo shoot I hated every single one of them for looking at you...for no doubt imagining what it would be like to make love to you... No one has a right to look at you like that but *me*.'

Nervously, Caitlin slid her tongue over her lips. 'What's the meaning of all this, Jake? What are you telling me?'

'I'm telling you that I want us to be lovers. I'm not saying I expect it to be forever but I want us to be together.'

'What you're saying is that if we get together you don't expect it to be a permanent arrangement?'

'Yes.'

The expression in his eyes looked haunted for a moment.

'The idea scares you?'

'I just don't trust that long-term commitment can ever really work. Look at the examples I've had.'

'You mean there's no chance you might be able to change that view? We've all been hurt, Jake…including me. After what Sean did to me it was never going to be easy to trust another man. If I can open my mind to the idea…can't you?'

He sighed. 'I'd like to tell you I could…but in all honesty I don't hold out much hope. I know myself too well.' He shook his head in frustration. 'Look, do things have to be so serious? Can't we just have some fun together?'

'I take it you're talking about sex? Is that how you see relationships, Jake as a chance to indulge in a little light-hearted sex with no commitment whatsoever?'

'No! You're taking everything the wrong way. Look, Caitlin, I'll respect you and take care of you for however long our relationship lasts…we'll enjoy whatever time we have together—that's all I meant. I only know that I want us to be up-front about things to everyone—not play cloak and dagger and pretend we aren't an item. After all, we're adults, aren't we?'

He seemed quite certain that their relationship couldn't last. Yes, his past had made him wary, and perhaps even *scornful* of any kind of commitment, but didn't he want to change that belief to something better? As much as she loved him, if Jake didn't have any faith that things could be different Caitlin wasn't going to settle. Her self-respect was paramount, and she wasn't about to risk losing it for even a second…not even for the man she loved.

'I'm sorry, Jake.' Pulling his jacket from her shoulders, she pushed it into his hands. 'If all you're offering me is some temporary little affair—some supposed "fun" until you grow tired of me and move on to somebody else—then I'm going to have to say no. You once asked me if I was sure I was committed to this band and I told you categorically *yes*. Right now that's all I'm interested in—the *band*. Now, if you'll excuse me, I really need to get back to my bed. If I don't get at least six hours' sleep then I won't be fit for anything tomorrow. Goodnight, Jake.'

Just before she turned and walked away Caitlin had the bittersweet satisfaction of seeing the bewilderment and hurt in Jake's eyes. But as she put more and more distance between them the pain she felt at knowing they would never be lovers again was so intense that she felt as if it drilled a hole right through her heart and out the other side.

Jake stayed where he was, staring out at the frigid sea for what seemed like an eternity. It was hard to take that Caitlin had turned him down. But then everything he'd wanted to say to her had somehow come out wrong.

His heart had leapt at her soft-voiced confession that she'd found it hard to trust another man after what her ex had done to her, and she'd given him a genuine opportunity to meet her halfway when she'd said that if she could open her mind to the idea of learning to trust again, why couldn't he? But he'd completely messed it up when he'd let fear take over instead. She'd been insulted that all he seemed to be offering her was a temporary affair.

Did she really believe that, given time, their association could become more permanent? Was she perhaps hoping for marriage?

He couldn't help it, but the idea of marriage made Jake's blood run cold when he recalled what Jodie had put him through. Caitlin was nothing like his mercenary ex-wife, but if she became well known, with all the temptations that fame would undoubtedly bring to a beautiful girl like her, wasn't it possible that *she* would be the one who grew tired of the relationship and wanted to move on to a better prospect? It would kill him to have to go through another bitter court battle if his new wife treated him in the same heartless way his ex had.

As he dug his now freezing hands into his jacket pockets and moved back down the pier Jake knew that as much as he cared for Caitlin, as much as he *desired* her and yearned to protect her, he couldn't risk losing his heart to her and having to endure the consequent fall-out should things go wrong.

Because if that happened, this time he really would be a broken man.

CHAPTER TEN

Planting himself at the back of the crowd that night, Jake sensed the familiar zig-zag of electricity shoot through him—as he always did before a band walked onto the stage…especially a band he was managing.

The day he stopped being excited about his work was the day he stopped living. He'd witnessed too many managers in the business become lazy or complacent when they got rich, content just to milk the financial rewards without actively contributing to a band's or a singer's success. Jake was scathing about such behaviour. For himself, music was its own reward—and if he could help a band attain success, then every sleepless night and grey hair was worth it.

Blue Sky was a week into their tour and the venue that night was a noisy and popular music pub on the Kent coast. The band were booked to play there from eight-thirty onwards. At Jake's suggestion they had made some last-minute alterations to the playlist, taking out a couple of the original tunes and replacing them with two slower numbers that Mike had written and that in Jake's opinion were outstandingly good. He was also showcasing Caitlin's skills as a vocalist.

On a more personal note, he loved to hear her sing those love songs—loved to hear the emotion in her voice that made all the hairs on the back of his neck stand up. Those performances sent shivers down his spine. *Not that he'd admit it to anyone—least of all to Rick, who seemed to be watching him like a hawk these days.* He couldn't exactly blame him. He was so sure that if Caitlin and Jake got together the result would be the break-up of the band.

Folding his arms across his chest, he released a frustrated sigh. He hated being in such a bind. But what the hell was he supposed to do? *Ignore* the feelings he had for her? The woman had got so deep into his blood that if he didn't get his daily fix of her he felt as if someone had died. If Jake hadn't know better he'd have sworn he was in—

Whoa. He reined in the thought with an accompanying sense of genuine panic.

'Good crowd tonight.'

Suddenly Rick appeared beside him, depositing a dark pint of real ale into Jake's hands with relish. Taking a deep draught of his own drink, he exhaled with pleasure, wiping the froth from his top lip with a grin.

'I've been told by the barman that this stuff is like nectar. It certainly beats that pint of warm dishwater masquerading as alcohol that I had last night.'

'I'll take your word for it.' Warily, Jake raised his glass to sample some of the dark brew for himself. As it slid down his throat the bitter taste of hops lingered unpleasantly in his mouth, confirming what he already knew to be true… he was no real ale aficionado. Give him a bourbon and Coke any day.

'So, how do you think things are going?' Rick asked, turning briefly to flash an irrepressible grin at a shapely blonde who'd walked by.

'So far so good,' Jake answered, his glance instinctively guarded. 'The band sounds great, and Caitlin's singing just gets better and better. We're going to be getting more great reviews…it's a given.'

'Man, I bless the day she walked into that musty old church hall and her voice blew us away. The gods were smiling on us that day, that's for sure.'

'I agree.'

'Hey, Jake, I hope you didn't take my advice about not getting involved with Cait too personally. I mean, we've been friends for a long time. We've never let a woman come between us before.'

'It was sound advice,' Jake replied soberly.

'Not that I blame you for being attracted to her. She sure is one beautiful woman, isn't she?'

Taking another reluctant sip of his beer, Jake remarked, 'You won't get an argument from me.'

The lights suddenly dimmed, and amid the tangible air of expectation that rippled round the audience the band walked onto the stage.

Jake's excitement was heightened along with everyone else's, but the smile on his face quickly turned into a frown when he saw what Caitlin was wearing. In place of the long skirts and silky tops she'd been favouring since they'd started the tour she was dressed in black bootcut jeans that hugged her hips like a second skin and a stretchy little white top that emphasised her eye-catching chest.

The males in the crowd weren't slow in demonstrating their appreciation. Jake did his best to try and shut out some of the more ribald comments. But with her flowing black hair, smiling green eyes and long legs, Caitlin was doing serious things to his blood pressure. He knew it was crazy, but he hated the mere idea that every red-blooded man in the room was fantasising about her. And underneath the hot, swift stab of jealousy that assailed him Jake felt a growing admiration for her daring. It seemed that Little Miss Hole-in-Her-Stocking was finally coming out of her shell.

Registering the looks of delight on the faces of the other band members as well as the crowd's, Caitlin launched into a mesmerising rendition of an iconic blues number and Jake silently acknowledged that her talent was astounding. As he watched her hips sway sexily to the music, her little white top riding up almost to waist level, he didn't think he'd ever felt so aroused or more hungry for a woman in his life.

* * *

Caitlin was quickly learning that after the almighty adrenaline rush of a live performance it was easy to crash down to the absolute depths shortly after. Now, alone in yet another hotel room—albeit a very luxurious one—with her room service supper left untouched on a tray, she sat in her pyjamas and robe with her head in her hands, feeling lonely and depressed.

An attack of the blues was the last thing she needed. But, as well as missing Jake's touch, the truth was that she was missing Lia—missing the easy camaraderie they shared. She also missed the buzz of working with her in the bookshop. Caitlin wasn't ungrateful for the privileged position she found herself in—actually living her dream of being a singer—but she'd be lying if she said she didn't miss the people and the place that she thought of as home.

Sighing, she reached for a magazine that was lying on the coffee table and decided to take it to bed with her. She was heading towards the prettily covered divan when there was a soft knock on the door. She opened it to Jake.

'Hi,' he greeted her. 'Can we talk?'

With her heart skipping a beat, she automatically stepped aside to let him enter. Her whole world immediately narrowed down to the force of his presence, her senses registering sensation overload with just one whiff of that sexy cologne he wore and one scorching glance from those extraordinary blue eyes of his.

Jake was a big part of the reason that Caitlin had crashed so low after tonight's performance. She still didn't really know where she stood with him, and the situation was making her as jumpy as if she was walking barefoot on tin tacks. One minute he was scowling at her and the next he was eating her up with his eyes. No wonder her nerves were stretched tight to the point of snapping.

Tonight he'd been very cool again, addressing her only when he had to, while in contrast Rick and the guys in the band had been elated with her performance and hadn't hesitated to show it. She was seriously perturbed that Jake seemed intent on giving her the cold shoulder. Had he decided that she was right about keeping their relationship a purely business one?

'You didn't eat your supper.' He glanced at the untouched tray of food balanced on the coffee table..

'I wasn't very hungry.'

'You have to eat to keep your strength up. Performing night after night can really take it out of you.'

'Thanks for your concern.' Making no attempt to couch the sarcasm in her tone, Caitlin raked her fingers through her recently washed hair, then caught the belt on her robe and wound it round her hand.

'Your performance tonight was wonderful. Anyone would think you'd been doing this for years. The others can't sing your praises enough.'

'And you?'

She barely managed to get the words past the ache in her throat. She ached to touch him, to drive that too serious expression from his haunting eyes and make him smile.

'If I started to tell you what I really think about you I wouldn't get back to my room tonight.'

His voice was huskily low, and every word he uttered sent inflammatory arrows of desire scudding crazily all over her body. Grabbing for a lifeline, Caitlin's gaze found and settled on the bottle of mineral water she'd ordered with her meal.

'Would you like a drink? It's only water, but—'

'I don't want a drink. I know I'm breaking all the rules here, but the truth is, Caitlin, I just can't stay away.'

His glance never leaving her face, he shrugged off his leather jacket and threw it onto a chair. Her mouth went dry at the sight of the hard, lean biceps that defined his upper arms in his black short-sleeved T-shirt. Startled, she focused on the dimple right in the centre of his chin—as usual his firm jaw was fashionably unshaven—but the dark shadow of beard didn't detract one jot from his heartbreakingly good looks. If anything, it simply added to the 'bad boy' persona he seemed to project without even trying.

'Well, you should,' she snapped. Turning on her heel, she unscrewed the top of the bottle of mineral water and took a swig. When she'd finished she turned back again and said, 'Because I don't want you here.'

Not commenting, Jake strolled across to the light switch and dimmed the overhead lights to a softly seductive glow.

Barely aware of what she was doing, Caitlin placed the water bottle back down on the tray. 'What are you doing?'

'I want you to come over here.'

'No.' But even as she answered in the negative she moved slowly towards him, as if she didn't have a will of her own...

When she was almost there she stopped and stared at him with desperation in her eyes. Jake opened his arms. In less than a second she'd closed the space between them to bury her face in the warm, musky scent of his T-shirt, registering the strong, steady throb of his heartbeat beneath the steely hardness of his chest. His hands fisted into her hair and he pressed her even closer against his body. Her heart was racing harder than it had ever raced before.

'Jake? Jake, I—' Raising her head, Caitlin stared into his smouldering gaze, want and need clawing at her as she registered the pure raw desire in his eyes.

Planting his palms either side of her face, he slanted his mouth hotly across hers to steal a hungry kiss that left them both stunned. With a groan she invited another kiss, her tongue intimately dancing with his, savouring the seductive flavours of bourbon and coffee and the hot, drugging sensuality that was uniquely *Jake*. Her hands slid down his back and lifted his T-shirt eagerly to trace the hard ridge of his spine with her fingertips. She was weak with wanting him, and when he backed up against the wall and deftly turned her in his arms, so that she took over his position, she allowed him to do it without so much as a murmur of protest.

'You know what I want to do?'

Her eyes widened in shock as well as anticipation as he expertly relieved her of her robe, then started to undo the buttons on her pyjama top.

'What?' Caitlin's voice was a barely-there bedroom rasp, because what Jake was already doing to her with his strong, sure touch and his drugging, sexy voice was nothing less than X-rated.

So much for years of trying to convince herself that her sex drive was low! Right now she didn't know how she wasn't just ripping his clothes off and taking what she wanted without hesitation. With a soft whimper, she briefly closed her eyes as he divested her of her top and feasted his hungry glance on her bared caramel-tipped breasts.

'I want to take you right here…and I want it to be hot and slow and deep…until we both go out of our minds with the pleasure.'

Even as Caitlin's heart beat wildly in her chest Jake lowered his head to claim her breast, drawing it deeply into his mouth. Bucking against him, she drove her fingers into the silky strands of his hair, crying out as ravenous need spiralled from her breast to her womb. He suckled and laved, teasing her rigid nipple with his tongue, then took her deep into his mouth again, his unshaven jaw sliding roughly cross her more tender skin, abrading her, marking her with his brand, leaving the trail of his scent all over her. Then he applied the same treatment to her other breast.

She was still quivering when Jake released her throbbing wet nipple and moved back up her body, with the wickedest smile she had ever seen. His pupils darkened to black as he settled his hands on the waist of her pyjama bottoms. With a firm tug, the silky fall of material shimmied down to her ankles. Her cheeks flushing heatedly, Caitlin watched him retrieve the protection he'd brought from his back pocket.

Her gaze immediately gravitated to his belt. He opened it to let his trousers slide down over his thighs and reveal his boxers. He loosened them, then ripped open the foil packet that contained the protection. He sheathed himself and Caitlin released a long, slow breath. Sliding her slender arms round Jake's neck, she pressed her body ardently against his. Immediately his hands moved to settle on the silky curve of her bottom, skimming her flesh and then pressing and kneading it until she was weak with want—until she thought she might die if he didn't take her soon.

Then he ravished her mouth again, before trailing hot damp kisses across her cheeks, her forehead, her eyelids, his clever hands stroking her body well past the point of no return, moving deftly to cup her in her most feminine place. Caitlin couldn't help but whimper his name, her lips pressing into the juncture between his neck and shoulder, kissing the warm masculine flesh with growing desire, taking lascivious little nips with her teeth...

Her body was primed to accept him. She knew she could no more prevent this act from reaching its logical conclusion than deny herself breath. Jake might be wary of commitment and find it hard to trust, but right then she impatiently pushed the thought aside—because she was greedy for his loving and would take anything she could get...*rightly or wrongly.* She would enjoy this time with him and revel in it. Revel in the fact that she was a sensual, desirable woman and that Jake was the only man in the world she wanted as her lover.

'Open your mouth,' he instructed, gravel-voiced and when she did he kissed her hard, sliding his hand beneath her bottom and raising her hips to the level of his. As her long, slender legs easily straddled him he plunged inside her with one sure, firm thrust, sending her world spinning off into another galaxy.

'Oh, Jake!'

Caitlin held on tight as he filled her again and again, each thrust more sure, more urgent, deeper than she could imagine, stealing kisses from her lips, her throat, her earlobe, until she thought she might die from the sheer dizzying pleasure of it.

'This is what I've been fantasising about doing all day,' he breathed against her neck, and at the same moment her world really did spin off its axis.

Jake quickly followed her. At the moment of climax he bucked hard against her, raggedly saying her name, the muscles in his toned hard body quivering like ropes of steel in the aftermath.

As his head fell forward onto her chest Caitlin drove her fingers through his tousled dark hair and had to bite her lip hard to stop herself from confessing that she loved him. *More than that, she wanted to marry him and one day have his children.*

Her certainty was so all-consuming that she thought surely Jake must sense it. But fear that all she would achieve by making such a confession might be to scare him away forever stopped her telling him. Jake had been a gypsy all his life, Rick had said, and probably always would be. What made her dare to hope for even a second that *she* could change his mind about that and help him see that they could still enjoy the pleasures of home and family?

'All right, everybody, time out. Cait? I'd like a word.'

Vaulting nimbly onto the small raised stage, Rick couldn't hide his exasperation as yet again Caitlin failed to come in at the right time on the intro.

Flushing a mortified pink, she turned round to shrug an apology to the rest of the band. To give them credit, they unanimously agreed that everyone was entitled to an off day now and then, and discreetly left the stage to her and Rick.

'What's going on with you this morning?' Rick didn't shy away from expressing his irritation. 'Didn't you get much sleep last night?'

She sighed. Sensing her cheeks burning at the accuracy

of Rick's innocent statement, she frantically thought of what she could say in answer.

To her surprise and delight Jake had spent the night. He had only returned to his room just as the sun came up—and then only reluctantly. Consequently neither of them had had much sleep...not when there had been far more exhilarating pleasures to occupy them. Caitlin knew she must have the dazed look of someone who'd burnt the candle at both ends. Her body still ached from Jake's passionate attentions and her concentration was all but shot to pieces.

Arriving for rehearsals at the intimate jazz club where they were appearing this evening, Rick had announced that Jake wouldn't be joining them until later and that until then he would be looking after things.

'I never sleep well in a strange bed,' she mumbled.

Rick's hazel eyes narrowed. 'You sure that's the reason?'

Agitatedly spearing her fingers through her hair, Caitlin sensed them tremble. Then she winced as she accidentally yanked out the silver hoop in her earlobe.

'What other reason would there be?'

'I don't know, babe...you tell me.'

She felt besieged—not to mention guilty...*guilty as hell.* Why couldn't Jake be around when she needed him? He would have taken charge of the situation in a second. She wasn't happy about lying to Rick about their relationship. With all her heart she wished they could be totally up-front about it, just as Jake had said he wanted to be.

'I don't know what you're getting at, Rick. I told you it would take me a while to get used to the change of lifestyle. It's hardly a crime that I'm feeling tired, is it?'

'No, it isn't.' Sighing heavily, Rick moved behind Caitlin and started kneading her shoulders. 'You're too tense. That's the trouble. Relax, can't you? Drop those shoulders. C'mon...listen to Uncle Rick.'

As jumpy as she was, she had to admit that what Rick was doing felt good...fantastically good. Right now her spine might have been made of concrete, she was so on edge, and anything to alleviate the tension had to be a step in the right direction. If she could only grab a couple of hours' sleep before the gig tonight she would be back on track again.

Dropping her head, she groaned as Rick's fingers applied some deeper pressure at a particularly tender spot between her shoulderblades. 'You're good at this, aren't you?' she murmured. 'You could have a whole new career, you know.'

'I must confess I've been told that before.'

Caitlin heard the smile in his voice.

'By one or two very grateful ladies who've succumbed to the pleasures of these hands.'

'You're quite the Casanova, aren't you?'

'Yes, well...if the cap fits.'

Her masseur halted his ministrations to drop a brief teasing kiss at the side of her neck... Unfortunately at the very same moment that Jake walked into the room.

The band's charismatic manager stopped dead in his tracks.

'Is this how you rehearse the band, Rick? Because if it is then we've got a serious problem on our hands...wouldn't you say?'

CHAPTER ELEVEN

WITHOUT REALISING IT Jake had clenched his hands into fists down by his sides. As he fought to corral his steadily growing temper his blazing blue eyes burned back at them both, his gut swirling with jealousy. *What the hell did Caitlin think she was playing at, allowing his best friend to fool around with her like that?*

Pink-cheeked and embarrassed, she stepped towards the edge of the stage. He wasn't surprised she was defensive.

'We *were* rehearsing, Jake. I just had a couple of problems Rick was helping me with.'

'Oh?' Jake's lip curled scathingly. 'Since when did I employ Rick as the group's masseur? Clearly I missed that.'

'For goodness' sake—the girl is tired! Tired and tense… I was just helping her iron out some of the kinks so that we could get on. The guys have gone outside for a break. I think I'll go call them back in.'

'No. Stay right where you are.'

His boot heels ringing ominously on the wooden floor, Jake strode towards the stage.

'We don't do anything else until I get to the bottom of this.'

With a horrible sinking feeling in the pit of her stomach, Caitlin jammed her hands into her jeans pockets and took a deep breath in. Was he jealous? Was that why he was so angry?

Her heart beat double-time, because she couldn't help noticing how gorgeous he looked. Dressed in fitted black jeans, a maroon shirt and a dark pin-striped suit jacket that flowed over his lean hard body as if it was tailor-made, he resembled one of those seriously unapproachable Italian models that featured in glossy magazines. His dark tousled hair and glittering blue eyes gave him a dangerous sexy edge and ensured there was nowhere else she'd rather look than at him.

'What are you talking about, Jake?' Rick jumped off the stage to confront the other man. 'You'd better explain.'

'I'm talking about you kissing her!' Jake glared at his friend.

Rick was bemused. 'I was just fooling around. You know me...I never could resist a pretty face.'

'That's a poor excuse for fondling my—'

'Go on... Your *what,* Jake?'

He'd been about to say my woman.

The realisation hit him hard—like a brick dropped on his head from a great height. As statements of ownership went, he couldn't have put it much more clearly. Here he was, standing head to head with his best friend and long-time associate, the pair of them like a couple of prize-fighters about to go into the ring. Jake cursed under his breath. He couldn't keep a lid on his temper, could he? He'd just had to let it out. Now he'd blown the whole situation wide open.

Rick's hazel eyes narrowed. 'You're sleeping with her, aren't you?'

Caitlin bristled indignantly. She most definitely didn't appreciate being discussed as if she wasn't there...as if she was some inconsequential possession rather than a human being. But as Jake glanced up and his heated glance locked onto hers it was as though he'd reached out and touched her. For a few debilitating seconds, her head swam.

'You just couldn't keep your hands off her, could you?' Rick's tone was scathing.

'Isn't that supposed to be *my* line?'

'Don't get cute with me, Jake! Just answer the damn question.'

With a terse shrug, the other man folded his arms. 'Yes. Caitlin and I are having a relationship. But don't start jumping to conclusions. It doesn't mean it's going to impact negatively on the band.'

'Is that right? Then how come we're at loggerheads? Answer me that. How long have we worked together? It's been a long time, Jake. In all that time we've barely had an angry word—and that's something in this business. Damn shame it has to happen now…and all because of a woman!'

'And just what's *that* supposed to mean?' Stooping down to climb off the stage, Caitlin dusted her hands and wiped them shakily on her jeans. 'In case you hadn't noticed I'm a person—just like you are. What is it with you and women, Rick? You like us well enough when it suits you, but something tells me you're deeply suspicious of our motives. Just to reassure you—I have no hidden agenda, and neither have I any intention of leaving the band. That being the case, you have no reason to doubt me. When I give my word, I keep it.'

'Right now, honey, it's not *your* word that I'm concerned about.'

'Okay, Rick… If you want to discuss this any further then you'd better meet me back at the hotel when we're finished here. I'm not prepared to stand around and lock horns with you when we're already eating into valuable rehearsal time. The band has a performance to give tonight and that's priority number one.'

With a brief glance down at his watch, Jake turned his attention to Caitlin.

'I want you to pull out all the stops tonight,' he told her. 'I didn't tell you before, because I didn't want to make you nervous, but there's going to be an A&R man from one of the big labels watching the show tonight. I can't make any promises, but if you and the band impress him enough there's a real possibility of getting a record deal. Kenny Swan knows that I don't back losers, and his interest has been snared by footage of you and the guys on social media over the past few nights. I'm counting on you—so don't let me down.'

Dumbly, Caitlin nodded. The possibility of the band gaining a recording contract so soon into their tour was nothing short of amazing. Yet right at that moment it paled into insignificance next to her unquenchable longing to be in Jake's arms.

She was relieved that he'd openly admitted to Rick that they were intimate, and she wanted the chance to show him that what they felt for each other could indeed flourish into something meaningful and lasting if they trusted their feelings and gave it a chance. At least now there would be no need to hide the fact that they wanted to be together, and she could really put her heart and soul into her singing.

Jake smiled. 'Work hard and I'll see you both later. I have a couple of important calls to make.'

'Jake?'

Suddenly finding her voice again, Caitlin stopped him in his tracks as he strode towards the back of the venue. Her anxious glance encompassed a scowling Rick as he leant back against the edge of the stage.

'I don't want you and Rick to fall out over this. My commitment is first and foremost to the band. I know you know that, but I just wanted to reiterate it.'

Jake's expression was as implacable as ever. 'I'm glad to hear it. Just concentrate on giving your best performance tonight and we might all come out on top.'

And with that he walked away.

He had the worst headache in living memory. The pain was so intense it had sent him hurrying down the narrow streets at half past five in the afternoon in search of a chemist.

Holding the packet of painkillers just a few minutes later, Jake ripped out two white tablets from the foil strip and swallowed them down with a warm can of cola. Grimacing, he threw the barely touched drink into a nearby wastebin and, biting his lip against the merciless throb in his temple, returned to his hotel.

Bolting his room door, he drew the curtains shut tight to blot out what was left of the daylight, then threw himself down on the bed and stared contemptuously up at the ceiling. *One thing was certain…he couldn't go on like this.* He only suffered migraines this bad when he was pushed into a corner, and his head was letting him know that right now he was probably jammed into the tightest corner he'd ever encountered.

There was no question that he wanted Caitlin. The situation between them wouldn't have developed if he hadn't. The electricity they generated between them could turn on the Christmas lights in Oxford Street without a power socket in sight. But lust was one thing and—dared he say it?—*love* was something else entirely.

He caught his breath, mulling the thought over.

Was love what he felt for Caitlin? If it was, then where did he go from here? In most people's books love meant commitment…the one thing he had always shied away from.

Jake was pretty sure now that what he'd felt for Jodie definitely *hadn't* been love. His decision to marry the woman had been crazy and it had cost him dearly. The truth was he had never committed himself properly to her. Wasn't that why he'd taken every opportunity to distance himself by travelling so often? She'd probably sensed his reticence at being with her long before she'd had her affair.

But what if the desire to escape reared its head again when he was with Caitlin? *He couldn't bear the thought that he might break her heart.* After the hell her ex had put her through she deserved someone who wouldn't cut and run. Someone who would support her journey as a singer. Someone who would be there when she needed them. Someone she could count on to stay around for more than just a few short weeks or months… In fact *someone the complete an-tithesis of himself.*

And now, to make matters worse, he had Rick on his case. When all was said and done his friend had every right to be furious with him. Jake had broken his own unwritten code about fraternising with band members and he'd potentially put the band at risk because of his fascination for Caitlin.

He would endeavour to put things right as soon as Kenny Swan from Lightning Records had seen the band perform tonight. If the man gave them a recording contract then hope-fully it would help Jake decide what he needed to do, and maybe then—*and it was a big maybe*—he would finally be able to have some peace.

'You can come? Lia, that's fantastic!'

Dropping down onto the bed, with its prettily embroi-dered quilt, Caitlin clamped her mobile firmly against her ear. To hear that her best friend was at last able to get away and come and hear her sing was the best news she'd had all day…next to the chance of Blue Sky getting a record deal, of course. But ever since that uncomfortable exchange between Jake, Rick and her at rehearsals that morning she hadn't been able to help worrying about what might happen next.

Rick's mood hadn't improved since Jake had left him in charge, and Caitlin feared for their friendship. *Was she to blame for their falling out?* If she was, then she would do her utmost to put things right. But in less than a couple of sentences Lia's cheery voice had managed to dispel her worry and doubt and replace it with a sudden rush of opti-mism and hope.

If Caitlin gave a good performance tonight—the *best* per-formance she'd ever given—the band might get that record deal, Jake and Rick's friendship might return to its previous status, and Jake might start to see that he and Caitlin had a future together outside of the band.

'I might be a little late if the traffic is bad,' Lia was saying, 'but I'll definitely be there. I've booked a room at that bed and breakfast you're staying at, like you suggested, so we'll be able to have a good old natter when we get back from the club. I'm so excited I can't wait! Hey—and you know what else?'

'What?'

Holding her hand out in front of her, Caitlin frowned at her chipped purple nail polish, wondering if she'd have time to repaint her nails before the gig tonight. It had to be right. Everything had to be right or it would be *her* fault if things went wrong. She was suspicious like that, and she wasn't taking any chances.

'I took a peek at your horoscope today,' her friend continued. 'Do you know what it said?'

'Go on.' There wasn't a muscle in Caitlin's body that didn't clench tight.

Lia took a deep breath in. 'Well, Saturn is meeting Venus today, and I'm sure you know that Venus is the planet of love and money? The timing is perfect. Saturn meets Venus beneath the auspices of the Mars/Jupiter rendezvous, so if you long for something in the money or romance stakes today's probably the time to ask for it. What do you think of that?'

Caitlin couldn't help but concentrate on the romance aspect. What would it take for Jake to see that she was serious about him? That she wanted to spend the rest of her life with him? That she'd go anywhere at any time with him and wouldn't regret a thing just so long as they could be together?

'Well, I've just been paid, so I'm okay for cash. As for romance, I…' She fell silent.

'Has something been going on?'

'What do you mean?' Leaning back against the plump pillows stacked against the padded headboard, Caitlin nervously wound a silken strand of burnished dark hair round her finger.

'Are you having an affair with someone in the band? Wait

a minute... I bet it's with the manager, Jake Sorenson.' Lia sounded emphatic. 'It's *him*, isn't it?'

'Next you'll be telling me that you're psychic.'

Smiling grimly at her own bad joke, Caitlin deliberately stalled for time. She had the beginnings of a headache and prayed that her friend wouldn't start giving her a lecture on the wisdom—or *lack* of it—in pursuing a relationship with Jake. Besides, it was far too late for her to start taking advice on *that* particular subject.

'That's not good news. It may or may not be deserved, but the man has a certain reputation after that scandal with his ex. Are you looking for trouble, or what? You're in a vulnerable situation as it is, and now you've gone and done possibly the worst thing you could do by getting involved with him! Oh, Cait...how *could* you?'

Shutting her eyes briefly tight, Caitlin slackened her hold on the phone, thought of Jake and the damage he could do to her heart with just a smile, and mused silently, *How could I not?*

'I've been looking for you.'

Jake.

At the sound of that familiar low-pitched voice Caitlin almost broke out in a sweat. Hanging her coat more securely on the old-fashioned peg in the dressing room, from which the garment had just slipped for the third time, she turned slowly round to face him. Her gaze made electrically charged contact with his.

'I popped out for some fresh air, but I've been here for about half of an hour,' she told him.

With its gilded French-style furnishings, including a sumptuous gold couch, a chaise-longue, two matching armchairs and a chic glass-topped coffee table, the room that had been designated for the band was full of old-style glamour, making it quirkily appealing and atmospheric. The walls were covered in photographs and posters of the bands and musicians who had played there over the years—some extremely well known—and Caitlin had already spent several minutes studying them and marvelling at how fate had brought her there to perform.

But her attention was no longer on the room. Jake's brooding presence was already making her feel feverish with need, and she didn't think she could be any more intimately aware of him if she tried.

'Rick's just gone to the bar to get you a drink.'

'Thanks.' She agitatedly twisted the silver bangle she was wearing, then pushed her fingers through her hair. 'It's far too hot in here...don't you think?'

He was smiling that roguish smile of his that could scramble her brain in a second and turn her limbs to damp strands of spaghetti.

'It's always hot when we're in a room together, Caitlin... Don't tell me you've never noticed?'

'Yes. Well...'

'By the way, you look sensational tonight.'

Jake's glance couldn't help but avidly home in on Caitlin's figure. She was dressed from top to toe in black—bootcut jeans that clung lovingly to her slender thighs and a slim-fitting shirt cut high on the waist that dipped just low enough to give him a tantalising glimpse of her delectable cleavage.

Just thinking about the taste of that satin-smooth flesh when he kissed her, he had to suppress the compelling urge to lock the door behind them and keep her captive. He hoped that Kenny Swan would appreciate the supreme sacrifice he was making in letting Caitlin go out there to sing tonight.

'I really hope there are no hard feelings between you and Rick.'

Jake shrugged. 'Rick and I will sort things out. We always do.'

A moment later he had shortened the distance between them. Reaching out, he laid his palm over her cheek. Soft as a newly opened petal, it beckoned him to touch again. As if anticipating the event, her plump lower lip quivered and the sight inevitably made his blood slow and thicken. Now he wanted to taste her, to plunder, to *brand*...

But he was swiftly denied the pleasure when Caitlin caught hold of his hand and lifted it firmly away.

'I need to talk to you, Jake.'

'After the gig tonight. We'll have a proper conversation then.'

'No. I need to tell you something now. I've got a friend coming back with me tonight. A friend from home.'

Disappointment, heavy and crushing, cramped his chest. 'Male or female?' he quipped jealously, straight away knowing that as a matter of principle he disliked the person already. *It didn't matter about the decision he ultimately had to make for both their sakes.* Right then, Jake wanted the dark-haired beauty in front of him exclusively for himself.

'It's Lia.' She shrugged a shoulder. 'The owner of the shop where I worked.'

'I remember...the one who had to have some wisdom teeth removed?'

Smiling wryly, Jake lifted a strand of Caitlin's hair and stared down at it, transfixed. Her green eyes widened.

'Jake? Is everything all right?'

Even as she asked the question dread coiled in the pit of her stomach. Somehow she knew that everything *wasn't* all right. There was something he wasn't telling her...something she was certain would cause her untold hurt...something she didn't want to know until she absolutely *had* to—because right then all she wanted to do was keep this man in her company until the last possible second...

'Stop worrying. Everything's fine.'

Jake had just bent his head to kiss her when Rick pushed opened the door and strode in. Depositing the tray of drinks he carried down onto the coffee table, his hazel eyes locked accusingly onto them both.

'Still taking care of business, Jake?' he commented sarcastically.

Even before Jake stepped out of their embrace Caitlin sensed his anger and irritation. Once again she put the blame for helping to create animosity between the two men squarely on her own shoulders.

'Don't blame Jake.' Lifting her chin, she unwaveringly met Rick's glance. 'It's my fault. I was the one who—'

'Save it, sweetheart.' His smile was resigned, but not unkind. 'You wouldn't be the first woman to become infatuated with Jake, and if I'm not mistaken you won't be the last.'

'I'd stop right there if I were you.' The cold glare that Jake directed at his colleague glittered like the sparkle of ice in a glacier.

'Why?' Rick demanded. 'Because you don't want her to hear the truth?'

'What truth?' Caitlin's mouth had already gone dry as sand.

'Jake doesn't have a particularly good track record with women. In this business not many men do...the temptations are often too great to resist. But, to be fair...' His glance focused even more intently on Jake. 'He *was* burned badly by his ex, and after that he swore never to commit to another woman again. I'd be very surprised if that view had changed. In any case, whatever he's told you, I wouldn't take it too seriously, Cait.'

The tension that rebounded between them deepened. In the pit of her stomach Caitlin felt sick, cold dread. Was he telling the truth? Was Jake intending to end their relationship before it had even really got started? Had she been painfully naïve in thinking that their passionate lovemaking really mattered to him? Jake had already made it clear that he wasn't offering her anything more meaningful.

What an idiot she was! When was she going to learn that some men were in the business of *taking*, not giving? Every time her ex Sean had told her that things would be different, that he would change, that they had a bright future together, she had believed him. Yes, she had even believed him when she'd bailed him out with the last five hundred pounds in her savings account, because he'd sworn to pay it back with interest. *Of course he never had.*

This wouldn't be the first time she'd been deceived by a man. But then, maybe *she* had done some of the deceiving. Hadn't she deceived herself when she'd believed that, given time and the chance to really get to know her, Jake might want to take their relationship more seriously? Her heart ached with renewed hurt when she realised finally that it wasn't true…could *never* be true.

'It's all right, Jake.' Even though her eyes had filled with tears, Caitlin faced him with an unflinching stare. 'Whatever you might think, I'm not as naïve as you imagine. We slept together, we made love…but deep down I never thought you intended to take things further. Don't worry. I'm not going to make a scene. And, despite what *you* might think, Rick, I'm not going to go to pieces because it's over between Jake and me. We'll still have a professional relationship…a good one, I hope. And now that that's clear I think I'll go and find the others and check in with them.'

She made a move to turn away.

'No—not like this, Caitlin.'

Jake scraped a frustrated hand through his hair. He was furious with Rick for putting him in such an untenable position. But he was also furious with himself—because now it looked as if he'd deliberately used Caitlin. *Nothing could be further from the truth.* He was crazy about her. Thinking of her practically consumed his every waking moment. What he felt for her was like nothing he'd ever experienced before, and the power of it took his breath away. And if he had trouble telling her that, then it was surely down to an inherent lack of trust that anything good could ever last?

Never in his life had he experienced feeling safe. Even as a small boy in the children's home he'd known that when he fell he fell alone. There would be no loving parent to pick him up and reassure him that everything would be all right.

Jake swallowed hard. Caitlin's beautiful emerald eyes were glistening with tears and in those few heartrending seconds he had never felt lower.

'I never meant to hurt you,' he breathed, lifting his hand to dry the moisture that tracked down her cheek.

She immediately backed away. 'Forget it.' Not giving him even the merest glance, instead she looked at Rick and enquired, 'Are the boys in the bar?' He nodded. 'Then I'll go and join them.'

She headed towards the door—but not before she heard him say to Jake, 'Just as well I'm around to pick up the pieces.'

CHAPTER TWELVE

JAKE COULDN'T BELIEVE that Caitlin had accepted a lift back to her guesthouse from Kenny Swan. The man was a smooth-talking Lothario, old enough to be her father. What on earth had possessed her? He had been all over her like a cheap suit, and if it hadn't been for the fact that Rick had pleaded with Jake not to make a fuss, because at the end of the gig Swan had offered them a lucrative contract, Jake would have put him straight about a few things.

As far as he was concerned a deal wasn't a deal until all the 'i's had been dotted and the 't's crossed, and he wasn't agreeing to a damn thing until he examined the details for himself...*preferably* under a microscope. He hadn't spent fifteen years working in the industry for nothing.

But right then, even though Blue Sky's good fortune should have been uppermost in his mind, it wasn't. *Caitlin* was. He could have strangled Rick for forcing the issue between them out into the open like that, without any regard for their feelings. No wonder Caitlin was mad at Jake. She had every right to be. And now he was suffering all kinds of agony, wondering if Kenny Swan had taken her straight back to her guesthouse or whether he had persuaded her to go home with him to his penthouse in Mayfair.

As far as pretty women went, rumour had it that the man had very few scruples. And it was little consolation to Jake to recall that Caitlin's friend Lia had been with her. He'd in-tuited that the blonde could easily take care of herself, and

Kenny wouldn't have hesitated to drop her off at the guest-house and then continue on to London with Caitlin, should she agree to the arrangement.

But even as he had the thought Jake knew that she *wouldn't*. She would never abandon her friend…she was far too loyal for that.

If only Jake hadn't been waylaid by the rest of the band, wanting to discuss the record deal, at the same time that Caitlin had been ensnared by Kenny at the bar, he would have persuaded her to go outside with him and get some fresh air. By the time he'd been able to return his attention to them Jake had seen that they were gone. He'd dashed outside, only to see the tail-end of Kenny's gleaming sedan with its tinted windows disappearing into the night—no doubt with Caitlin seated snugly beside him while her little blonde girlfriend sat in the back.

'I thought you could probably use this.' Rick placed a steaming cup of black coffee on the bar and pulled up a stool next to Jake.

The venue was slowly emptying of late-night revellers who'd watched the band and were clearly reluctant to go home. Behind the two men bar staff were methodically clearing tables and stacking chairs. A mournful-sounding love song was playing softly in the background, and Jake couldn't help but feel despondent. The relentless longing for Caitlin that had taken up residence in his heart didn't abate, and he knew it was serious. The mere idea that she might walk away and find somebody else was simply not to be tolerated. *It dawned on him then that he'd move heaven and earth just to be with her…*

'Thanks.'

'I scrounged it off a pretty barmaid…charmed her with my good looks and irresistible wit.'

'Now, there's a surprise,' Jake commented drolly.

The two men fell silent for a while.

As if disturbed by the gloomy expression that flitted across his friend's features, Rick remarked consolingly, 'Kenny's probably just dropped her off at the guesthouse. Cait's a clever girl. If he tries anything she'll soon put him straight.'

'You think? But I could hardly blame her if she *did* go home with him, could I?' Jake stared grimly down into his coffee.

'You really care about her, don't you?'

There was a tone of genuine surprise in the other man's voice.

'Is that so hard to believe?'

'I'm sorry, buddy. I just—'

Jake sighed. 'What I felt for Jodie all those years ago wasn't love, Rick. I was just tired of being alone and I kidded myself she was important to me in the ridiculous hope that my feelings might grow fonder. Needless to say, when I realised she only wanted me for what she could get, they *didn't*. As things turned out…I'm glad about that. I'd rather she took my money and everything I possessed than broke my heart. That's a pain I couldn't get over so easily.' Grimacing, he shook his head. 'But what I feel for Caitlin is… Well, it's like nothing I've ever experienced before. I already know she's got the power to break my heart.'

'Sounds to me like it's love, Jake.'

He didn't dispute the fact. For a few heartfelt moments he let the thought settle.

'Look, I know I should put the band first, but to tell you the truth I've been thinking about resigning as manager and asking you to take over. I was thinking I should get out while the going's good and limit any disappointment and ill feeling it might cause. Things are really starting to take off for Blue Sky, and you know exactly what to do to maximise their potential and take them right to the top. They trust you, Rick. You'll all be just fine without me.'

'Why would you want to resign, Jake? Is it because you're afraid of hurting Cait?'

'She deserves this chance just as much as the others do. What she *doesn't* deserve is for me to screw it up because I've become personally involved with her. I don't know if I'm capable of maintaining the necessary professional detachment any more. I feel like a house of cards that's been knocked down. It's not like me to lose my head over a woman. But since falling for Caitlin I can't eat, I can't sleep, and my concentration feels like it's been blown apart by a scatter gun. At this rate I'm not going to be much use to anyone—let alone myself.'

With a rueful grin, Jake raised his coffee to his lips.

It was Rick's turn to sigh. 'Trust me, resigning isn't the answer. Cait wouldn't want that, and nor would the guys. And *nor*, for that matter, would I. If you want her then go after her, man! What are you sitting here for? If she *has* gone back to Kenny's—'

'I thought you said that wasn't likely?'

Jake's cup clattered against the saucer and hot black coffee sloshed messily over the side. He was suddenly seized by the most terrible doubt. *Would* Caitlin have been persuaded by Kenny to go home with him? What if she had agreed in order to teach Jake a lesson?

'Hey, slow down. Of course it's not.' Rick said. 'Look, I'm sorry if I haven't been as supportive as I could have been. I guess I'm just very protective of the band. I'll just have to accept the fact that you and Cait are an item now. Having got to know her a little, and knowing you like I do, I'm sure you won't let your relationship damage the band in any way. To tell you the truth, I'm glad you've finally found someone you really care about. In my opinion, you couldn't have found anyone better than Caitlin. She's pretty special. If you really want to check that she's okay why don't you drive over to the guesthouse and see if you can talk to her?' he exhorted.

Moved by his friend's support, and clutching at a ray of hope he perhaps had no right to cling to, Jake glanced down at his watch.

'It's two in the morning, Rick. I booked her into a guest-house because she said she didn't want to stay in another soulless swanky hotel, and the place is run by a landlady who's about as friendly as Attila the Hun. When I booked the place that reassured me. She keeps strict hours and she likes her guests to be back before midnight. The prospect of banging on her door at this hour of the night just so that I can tell Caitlin I—'

'Love her?'

The grin hijacking his friend's face was wide. Jake scowled. Then he drove his hands agitatedly through his hair.

'Is that what you call this perpetual longing and needing and climbing the walls when I can't be with her?'

The other man nodded knowingly.

Inside Jake's chest his heartbeat stumbled at the realisation that he'd allowed Caitlin to believe that his attraction to her was purely physical. *He'd been seriously kidding himself.* Now he knew that he'd put her happiness and wellbeing way above his own. That was why he'd told Rick he was willing to resign as the group's manager.

He blew out a long, slow breath. 'Then I guess you're right. But if she thinks that means us moving in together into some detached mock-Georgian in the suburbs then we're likely to have our first real fight. I couldn't do it. That's why I've never settled anywhere. I'm a born gypsy. I get too restless to stay in one place for long…you know that.'

'Yeah, and I also know that you haven't even asked the lady what she wants yet. First you need to tell her that you love her. Caitlin's a great girl, Jake. She's as passionate as you are and she loves the band. She loves singing. Do you think she would have auditioned if she'd wanted to settle for some safe little existence in the suburbs? I hardly think so.'

Glancing back at Rick, he felt the ray of hope that had surfaced earlier suddenly grow much brighter.

'Hey, if you ever get tired of being on the road I could see you winding up as some sort of relationship counsellor.'

'You think so?'

'No, I don't.' To Rick's consternation, Jake lightly punched him on the shoulder and laughed. 'Not in a million years.'

'That aside, what are you going to do about Cait? Are you going to try and see her tonight?'

'No… Not tonight. It's been a tough few days and she needs her rest. I'll just have to trust she went back to the guesthouse with Lia and go and see her in the morning. In the meantime…' He reached into his back pocket to retrieve his mobile, 'I'll send her a text…just to check.'

'Sounds like a plan. Now that's settled, how about a *real* drink?'

Signalling to one of the barmaids, Rick gave her one of his incorrigible smiles and looked hopeful.

Having ordered a latte and a blueberry muffin, Caitlin stared out through the café window at the frigid purple and grey sky that definitely heralded rain. It didn't particularly disturb her. She couldn't feel much gloomier than she did already.

The impersonal little text she'd received last night from Jake had hardly been reassuring.

Hope you enjoyed last night's gig and got back to the guesthouse OK. I'll catch up with you in the morning.

He hadn't even included an 'x' to denote a kiss.

But then she knew she had played her part when she'd stupidly accepted a lift from Kenny Swan without even telling him. She'd done it because Jake had been busy talking to the rest of the band and she had felt inexplicably jealous. *Ignored.* She knew it was ridiculous, because he *was* the group's manager, but right then she hadn't wanted to share him with anyone. Even Lia's reassuring presence hadn't consoled her.

The news about the recording contract was wonderful, but her pleasure was sadly tainted by the hurtful realisation that the man she loved didn't love her back.

'Cheer up, love, it may never happen.' The handsome young assistant who had taken her order returned with her coffee and cake.

'What did you say?' She glanced up at him, not comprehending.

'You looked sad…I was just trying to cheer you up. Anyway, enjoy your coffee.' With a cheeky wink and a tuneless whistle, he returned behind the counter.

Discovering that she'd suddenly lost all desire for cake, and after taking just a few sips of her coffee, Caitlin scraped back her chair, left the money for her bill on the table and hurriedly left. *How could she possibly eat when all she could think about was Jake?*

'Where have you been?'

He was waiting outside the guesthouse when she returned and the expression on his face was as implacable as ever. Steeling herself against the blast of icy wind that suddenly hit her, Caitlin shoved her long hair out of her eyes and stared.

'It's nice to see you, too,' she murmured..

'I was worried about you. I even got your landlady to check your room—which was no easy feat, I can tell you. She told me that your bed was made but she couldn't tell whether you'd slept in it or not.' Stepping towards her, he frowned. 'What's going on, Caitlin?'

'Nothing… I just went for a cup of coffee, that's all.'

'So you *did* sleep in your bed last night?'

'Of course I did.'

'Why didn't you reply to my message asking if you were Okay?'

'It was two o'clock in the morning when you sent it—that's why. I was tired and I fell back to sleep. Wait a minute...where did you think I'd slept if it wasn't in my bed at the guesthouse?'

'You were eager enough to go off with Kenny.'

'The man offered us a lift, and because you seemed busy talking to Rick and the others I accepted. I was tired, Jake. I'm still a novice at this game and I expend a lot of energy trying to get it right.'

'You're doing just fine, Caitlin. In fact you never cease to amaze me with how dedicated you are in giving a great performance. Last night you were flawless. You knocked it out of the park!'

'Thanks.'

Her smile was guarded and a flash of pain squeezed at Jake's heart. *Had he pushed her too hard?* He'd hate to think she wasn't deriving any pleasure from singing with the band any more.

Making a concerned examination of her features, he noticed for the first time that she was unusually pale, and beneath her lovely green eyes he could see bruising shadows.

'We should talk,' he said quietly.

'Not right now. I need to go inside and pack and say goodbye to my friend. She'll be wondering where I am. I didn't wake her to let her know I was going out.'

She moved towards the steps that led up to the house's front door. Jake stared in disbelief. Then he came to his senses and caught hold of her arm.

'Are you trying to hide something from me, Caitlin?'

'What do you mean?'

'Tell me the truth. *Did* you stay at Kenny's place last night?' He was unable to hold back his fury at the thought.

Her green eyes flashed.

'I already told you that I didn't. The man is a snake. I

know he wants to sign us, but if the agreement means he has some unspoken right to make suggestive remarks to me whenever he gets the chance then you can find another singer—and I don't say that lightly. I love this band, and I want it to do well. But I've played the part of sacrificial lamb before, and I'm damn sure I'm not going to play it again. Not for anybody!'

'Did he insult you? Hurt you?' Jake's voice was a gravelly undertone.

He could hardly believe that he'd put Caitlin in such a vulnerable position. When he saw Kenny Swan again he'd have to be physically restrained from connecting his fist to his jaw…contract or no contract. And he was pretty sure the rest of the crew would feel the same.

'Of course he didn't. Apart from making me cringe at some of the comments he made about his sexual prowess and inviting me to join him in his hot tub he didn't try anything. Anyway, Lia was with me,' she answered. 'Plus, like I told you before, I'm tougher than I look. Lucky for me I wear any bruises I acquire on the *inside*.'

The idea that he might be responsible for some of those invisible bruises affected Jake more deeply than he could say.

'I'm sorry. But you should never have agreed to let him drive you home. You should have come to get me and I would have taken you and Lia back to the guesthouse straight away. Now, why don't you go and say goodbye to Lia, then come back to my hotel with me?'

Caitlin couldn't easily hide the resentment that flashed through her. She pulled her arm free and rubbed it.

'What would be the point, Jake? If you want to talk about our relationship then there's really not much to discuss, is there? Why prolong the agony? We had an affair…a meaningless affair. It happens all the time—especially in this business. You of all people should know that.'

'Meaningless? Is that what you think this is?'

Jake hated hearing her talk like that…as if he made a habit of sleeping with different women just because he could. He'd never been a saint, but neither was he promiscuous— despite what the gossip columns might have suggested over the years.

For the first time since he'd acknowledged his feelings about Caitlin to himself Jake was forced to consider that perhaps she didn't feel as intensely as he did. The thought was so unpalatable that it hit him with all the force of an express train travelling at full speed. Suddenly being uncertain of his ground shook him badly.

'Like I said, you've made your feelings about me pretty clear.' She sighed. 'It was me that clouded things with my stupid hopes and dreams. You'd think I would have learned after Sean, wouldn't you? Anyway, the band is the most important thing…not whatever's going on between you and me. At least we're agreed on that.'

Twisting her hands together, Caitlin managed a tremulous smile just before she turned away.

If I can just hold it together until he goes, she thought, then I might…just might…get through this with my pride and dignity intact. And I might stop him from ever finding out that he's the only man who has my heart and always will…

'You're wrong, you know.'

Still with her back to Jake, Caitlin released a weary sigh. 'Wrong about what?'

'The band *isn't* the most important thing to me.'

She froze. Then she slowly turned round to find him wearing a smile that was uninhibitedly warm and sexy, and it drove every single thought out of her head. His twinkling glance fused to hers and she couldn't have looked away even if she'd wanted to. As her body was suffused with unexpected heat even the icy wind swirling round them seemed suddenly to grow less frigid.

Her mouth drying, she asked, 'It isn't?'

'No, it isn't. *You* are, Caitlin. You're the most important thing in my life. I'm not proud of the way I've handled things between us, but to say I've never felt like this before would be the understatement of the century. An earthquake couldn't have shaken me up more.'

'I wondered where you'd got to, Cait. Now I see what's delayed you.'

The front door opened to reveal the diminutive Lia, dressed in pink sweatshirt and jeans, her brown eyes alighting on Jake as if she'd inadvertently stumbled upon the devil incarnate.

'What's *he* doing here? Unless he's come to talk to you about work then I think you should tell him to go. He'll only upset you, and you've had enough grief from him already to last you a lifetime.'

'Hang on a minute, Lia, I—'

Caitlin was cut short when the blonde hurried down the steps and pushed her aside to plant herself in front of Jake. With her hands on her hips, she proceeded to tell him exactly how she felt.

'She broke her heart over you last night, Jake Sorenson. She cried like the rain. I've never seen her cry like that since she was with Sean—and he took her for a ride too, making promises he never intended to keep. I *told* her you'd break her heart. Well, I hope you're feeling proud of yourself. And then, if your own conduct wasn't bad enough, you go and leave her in the clutches of that middle-aged Lothario, reeking of enough cologne to sink a battleship! Thank heaven I was with her last night or God only knows what might have happened. If you and he are an example of the kind of people in the music industry then Caitlin would be better off singing at our local pub on a Saturday night. At least she'd be safe.'

Shock jack-knifed roughly through Jake at the thought that he hadn't protected Caitlin when he should have, and regret that he'd caused her even a moment's pain. He could see how the situation must appear to Lia, and he'd be the first to admit it didn't look good. It was a crying shame that his reputation preceded him, because no matter how he behaved he was damned—in the blonde's eyes at least And Kenny Swan's conduct didn't exactly create the best of impressions either.

He fixed the girl with a steely glare.

'Please don't slot me into the same category as Kenny Swan. At least spare me *that* particular insult. I assure you that Blue Sky won't be dealing with him again. More to the point, I'll ensure that Caitlin deals with someone else at the record company. There are plenty of genuinely good people who work there. As for the rest—I think that's between Caitlin and me...don't you?'

'Caitlin?' Her brown eyes glinting like a protective mama bear's, Lia folded her arms and looked round at her friend for confirmation.

Caitlin nodded. 'I'd like to have a few minutes alone with Jake. I think it's needed.'

'Just as long as you don't let him persuade you to do anything you don't want to do. You've got free will, remember? You got over Sean and you can get over *him* too.'

With a warning glance at a bemused Jake, Lia sprinted back up the stairs and went inside the house.

'Does she always behave like an aggrieved matador about to pick a fight with a bull?' he asked dryly.

Caitlin's smile was tentative. 'For some reason she's very protective of me.'

'I'm glad.'

Although in future Jake wanted to be the one doing all the protecting. He knew that now—knew it without a single doubt. The thought was exhilarating...like a hang glider hitting a warm air thermal. All he had to do now was convince her that he was in earnest.

'Will you come back with me to the hotel for a while? I'd really like to say what I have to say to you in private.'

Smoothing her hand down the front of her raincoat, Caitlin sucked in a steadying breath.

'I have something I want to say to you too, Jake. But I'm not waiting until we get back to your hotel. It's better said out here, in the open. You've told me that I'm important to you, but the truth is…the truth is I don't know if I can be enough for you.'

She swallowed hard, her cheeks glowing a little with embarrassment.

'What about the next pretty girl who becomes infatuated with you? You like your lifestyle just the way it is. You don't want to commit yourself to one person and I don't want anything less.'

There…she'd finally said it. She'd put her cards on the table and the consequences be damned.

'Is that what you think? That you're not enough for me?'

To Caitlin's consternation, he laughed out loud.

'I don't know if I could handle you if you were any more woman than you are already, but I'd willingly die trying! What's all this talk about not being enough? Caitlin, you're my fantasy come to life—my most heartfelt dream come true. Why would I be remotely interested in any other woman? It's true that there will always be pretty women in this business, but that doesn't mean I'll be remotely interested. Why would I if I have you? In any case, most of my time and energy goes into my work, and that's the way I've wanted it…up until now, that is.'

With a meaningful pause Jake allowed his gorgeous blue eyes to reflect a promise that Caitlin hardly dared believe.

He continued. 'And now I'm planning on using some of that time and energy in keeping you one very happy and contented woman, Caitlin Ryan…for the rest of your life.'

'What are you telling me, Jake?' She still wasn't convinced of the startling equation her fevered brain had helplessly arrived at.

'Is it really so hard to comprehend?' He smiled, 'I'm asking you to marry me.'

'You're serious?'

Her breath caught on a gasp. She was giddy and light-headed at the same time, just as if she'd been spinning on a carousel.

'I'm perfectly serious.'

Jake purposefully covered the short distance between them and took hold of Caitlin's hands in earnest.

'Don't you get it? I love you and I want you to be my wife. I think you already know what a nomadic life this is, being on the road with a band…it's never going to be a conventional lifestyle. I'd be lying to you if I said it would be.'

'That's a relief, because that wouldn't suit me at all. I'm a bona fide rock chick now, remember? I have my reputation to consider.' Caitlin's smile was uninhibitedly warm. 'Home will always be wherever we are together, Jake. There's a big wide world out there and I want to see some of it. If you're willing, you could show me, couldn't you?'

'I can't think of anything I'd like more.'

Suddenly impatient, Jake pulled her into his arms and planted a hot, hungry kiss on her mouth. He heard the soft helpless moan she breathed as he gently withdrew. Drawing the pad of his thumb down over her cheek, he was deeply satisfied to see the mutual desire and longing that her pretty green eyes reflected back at him.

'But I don't want you to think that I'm not open to compromise regarding a more permanent home,' he told her. 'Eventually I'd like us to have children…buy a place in the country, maybe? A place where they'll have plenty of space to play and grow up.'

Caitlin couldn't help but be moved by his heartfelt declaration. To hear Jake say that he wanted them to have children, that he was more than willing to embrace the prospect and ensure that his own children did not have a lonely childhood bereft of family or siblings like he had done… Well, it was *beyond* wonderful.

She sighed. 'I love you, Jake…I love you with all my

heart. There's no one I'd want to be the father of my children but you. Do you really want to marry me?'

'Right now I can't think of anything I want more than for you to be my wife. Except perhaps to have you naked in my bed.'

'And us being married—it won't cramp your famous rock and roll lifestyle?'

Jake grimaced. 'The so-called rock and roll lifestyle isn't all it's cracked up to be. For one, it's bloody lonely out on the road for weeks at a time, and after a while one hotel room looks much the same as another...whether it's in Islington or Istanbul. I'm never going to be a conventional nine-to-five husband, Caitlin, but I'll always be there for you when you need me. That's a promise.'

'Then I suppose my answer to such a sincere and heart-felt proposal has to be yes.'

'Yes, what?'

Lia put her head impatiently round the door, her chin jutted warningly towards Jake.

Grinning, Caitlin told her. 'Jake has just asked me to marry him.'

Lia's face was a picture. Tussling between giving them both a lecture and fighting the urge to smile, because of the way Jake's twinkling blue eyes were all but devouring her friend, she concluded that it would be a crime against passion for the two of them *not* to get married.

'Oh. I suppose that's all right, then.'

Jake's eyebrows flew up. 'You mean we have your permission?'

'You know very well that Caitlin doesn't need my permission.' With an irritated huff, Lia stepped out to survey them properly. 'But when you care about people you naturally want what's best for them.'

'I agree.' Glancing towards her, he said clearly, 'I love your friend, Lia. And, if you'd be so kind as to leave us alone together for a while, I won't hesitate to demonstrate the fact.'

The neatly painted front door of the guesthouse closed behind Lia with an obliging click.

As Jake's mouth descended avariciously on Caitlin's lips a profound sense of coming home rolled over her. The sensation was so powerful and so warm that she knew to the depths of her soul that there was no more room for doubt or mistrust. She was no longer a displaced person, aching for someone to love who would unreservedly love her back.

She'd grown in confidence since joining Blue Sky, and wherever her journey as a singer took her everything would be all right—because Jake would be there with her, loving her and rooting for her all the way...her husband, her manager, her friend—and, one day, the beloved father of her children.

Long seconds later Jake broke off their kiss to gaze deeply into Caitlin's eyes. 'There's just one small snag,' he said seriously.

'Oh? What's that?'

'You *do* know that we're probably going to have to contend with Rick singing a solo at the wedding?'

'Is there any way we can divert him?'

'We can always ask Tina, the barmaid at the Pilgrim's Inn, if she'd help us out.'

'Do you think that she would?'

'How could she *resist?*'

They were still laughing as they ascended the guesthouse steps, intent on sharing a celebratory drink with Lia.

* * * * *